D1625145

T

THE
TRAMPLED
FIELDS

Other Five Star Westerns
by Jeanne Williams:

Beneath the Burning Ground Book I:
    The Underground River
Beneath the Burning Ground Book II: The Hidden Valley

BENEATH THE BURNING GROUND
BOOK III

THE
TRAMPLED
FIELDS

A FRONTIER STORY

JEANNE WILLIAMS

Five Star • Waterville, Maine

First Edition
First Printing: March 2005

Published in 2005 in conjunction with
Golden West Literary Agency.

Set in 11 pt. Plantin.

Printed in the United States on permanent paper.

Library of Congress Cataloging-in-Publication Data

Williams, Jeanne, 1930–
    The trampled fields : a frontier story / by Jeanne Williams.
    —1st ed.
        p. cm.—(Beneath the burning ground; bk.3)
    ISBN 1-59414-121-5 (hc : alk. paper)
    1. Kansas—History—Civil War, 1861–1865—Fiction.
2. Frontier and pioneer life—Fiction.   I. Title.
PS3573.I44933T73 2005
    813′.54—dc22   2004028105

For JUNE WYLIE

Dear friend for many years,
who probably saw more obscure parts
of eastern Kansas than she cared to.
Her indulgence contributed greatly
to this story's sense of place.

CHAPTER ONE

Hildy added a double handful of cracked hickory nuts to the peas, corn, beans, and venison stewing in the pot hung over the fire and gave the Tom-fuller a stir. There was a big washing to do, but dinner would take care of itself now except for making ashcakes. She made them with plenty of molasses. Her husband, Justus, before he had been sold away, used to say they were better than his mama's—not where his mama would hear, of course. Aunt Becky, as Justus's mama was known, already had had grudges aplenty toward her daughter-in-law.

"Puttin' on airs 'cause Miss Lou raised you in the big house after your ma died," Aunt Becky often had sniffed. "Taught you alongside her own young 'uns till they went off to school. While my girls and Justus worked, there you was with your nose in a book, or sewin' with Miss Lou."

After Hildy's mama had died, it had been Miss Lou who had said: "Don't be scared, honey, Master Richard and I will take care of you. You're going to sleep in that little room next to ours." It had been Miss Lou who had come in softly, at night, to make sure Hildy was covered up, and who started her in primer with Master Edmund who was just her age then, five. Miss Alice had been three years older and could write a beautiful hand and cipher in her head fast as lightning. That had made Master Richard chuckle and say that before long she could straighten out his careless records.

Hildy's throat tightened. Master Richard had laughed a

lot, gray eyes shining like he found the world so full of joy he was about to bust with it. Except when he flew into one of his rages. No one could do anything with him then, not even Miss Lou.

It had been in a fit like that he had sold Justus off to that Missouri bishop just a few months after he himself and Miss Lou had given them a wedding—a real wedding in the dining room with Parson Douglas, and a fine dinner served on the good china on a damask tablecloth, not just a moving in together with the master's approval and a jollification.

None of that had signified when Master Richard Frazer had taken Justus to task because a favorite mare had gone lame and he had thought Justus hadn't shod her properly. Justus had reminded his master that he'd warned him the mare had thrush in the frog of her hoof that needed to be cleaned and treated every day till it healed.

The veins had swelled in Master Richard's forehead. "Are you talking back, you insolent nigger?"

"No, Master Richard, but. . . ."

That had set Master Richard off, probably because he had known he should have made sure the stable help doctored the hoof. It had wound up with the first whipping Justus had ever got—not enough to break the skin bad but enough to make him swear he'd run away.

"I'm a good smith," he had growled while a sobbing Hildy salved the welts. "I'll save up to buy you, or, if that takes too long, I'll just come back and take you North."

Before he could find a good time to run, that bishop had passed through, needing a smith. Hildy had heard Miss Lou pleading, but Master Richard had told her to say no more. He wouldn't tolerate an insubordinate servant.

White folks at Waverly had never said "slaves". It was hands or servants or "our black people". When Hildy had begged to be sold along with her husband, Master Richard had upbraided her for ingratitude. Then he had tried to console her. "The new smith I'm getting, Hildy, is of amiable temper and fine-looking. He needs a wife."

She hadn't understood for a moment. When she had, it had hurt worse than a whipping. What Master Richard had meant was a slave's marriage didn't count. She purely had hated him for a heartbeat, although she had grown up worshiping him almost as much as she had Miss Lou.

"I'm married to Justus, Master Richard," she had said when she could speak. "By the parson. You watched with your own eyes."

The pupils of those eyes had swelled like he was going into a fury. Women weren't whipped at Waverly, but she could have been the first. When he had spoken, though, his voice had been controlled and she had known he wouldn't change his mind. "Your marriage is annulled as of this minute. I won't force you to take another husband, Hildy, but you'll stay here because your mistress relies on you."

Miss Lou, at forty-three, had been in the family way. It had happened pretty often when a woman neared the end of her childbearing years. One more bitterness. Hildy and Justus hadn't started a baby, never would. For Bishop Jardine had written how Justus had run off a few months after he was fetched up to Missouri—asked Master Richard to watch out for him in case he tried to get back to Waverly and see Hildy.

He hadn't. Not in five long years. The way North was dangerous. Hildy feared he might be dead, but refused to have another man. She had loved Justus ever since they were thirteen, when he'd rescued her from a drunken overseer. Master Richard had horsewhipped the white man and run him off the place.

9

The recollection softened Hildy, brought back a rush of good memories of Master Richard. He had called in doctors if any of his folks were bad sick; old folks were taken good care of till they died; he gave four full holidays in the summer and a week at Christmas with new clothes and a feast for everyone.

Most of all, there was that light, bright heart in him. How he'd grab Miss Lou off her feet, swing her around, and hug her while she'd blush and laugh and scold! Aunt Becky had grumbled about that, too. "Married twenty years and still carryin' on like they just laid eyes on each other!"

No one would lay eyes on Master Richard again. Killed three months ago at Wilson's Creek up in southwest Missouri on August 10, 1861. *Our Cherokees captured all save one of the enemy's artillery pieces,* his colonel had written, *thus assuring a Confederate victory. Your brave husband, madam, died attempting to take that last Union howitzer. May pride in him and the cause he died for be of solace and know that all here grieve the loss of their gallant captain. I assure you that he is decently buried.*

Miss Lou hadn't smiled since then except when little Master Richie climbed into her lap, gripped her face between his palms, and commanded: "Laugh, Mama! Richie wants to hear you!"

She would, a little, then call him her big boy, and gather him close as she buried her face in his hair, curly gold like his father's. Very winning was Master Richie. At first, Hildy had succeeded in hating him, blaming him for her not being sold along with Justus, blaming him because she couldn't have a baby of her own. She'd changed him and bathed him and walked him, when he cried and Miss Lou was too tired to cosset him, but she hadn't crooned to him or cuddled him, had hardened her heart against his tiny perfect fingers, the pulse beat of that soft spot in his skull.

I could drop him. . . .

The wicked thought had scared her into being extra careful, but she still hadn't touched him one bit more than she had to. Then Miss Lou's breasts had caked. She had wept when she tried and failed to nurse the baby, suffering something terrible in spite of the hot poultices Aunt Becky put on her. The doctor had lanced her breasts, and her fever had dropped, but her milk had dried up.

The baby had sucked his sugar tit and wailed high and shrill with hunger. Out of the fifty slaves in the cabins and big house, there had been only two nursing mothers. Each had tried to suckle Master Richie, but Ruby's milk had been too rich—gave him colic—and Amelia's nipple had been so small he kept losing it. Richie hadn't had the strength to howl, had just mewled like a kitten. The nearest plantation was that of the Cherokee chief, John Ross. Master Richard had sent to hire or borrow a wet-nurse, but it would have been hours before one could come, hours that the poor little scrap might not have been able to last.

Had he been Master Richard's by another woman, Hildy might have told herself it was no sin to let nature take its course. The helpless infant might well grow into his father's rages. But the babe was Miss Lou's, had cost her mightily— and he was so hungry.

"Wait, Amelia." Hildy had motioned the young woman back into a chair and got a bowl. "See if you can't squeeze some milk in here."

Once Amelia had gotten the hang of it, she quickly had the bowl half full of thin bluish milk. "Good!" Hildy had praised her. "Let's see if this works."

Cradling Richie, she had soaked the muslin sugar tit in the milk and poked it in his mouth. He had sucked greedily,

delving his fingers into her breast. Hildy had felt an odd
sensation beneath his hands, as if the veins were engorging.
He nearly emptied the bowl before he drowsed off with the
first content stomach he'd had in days.

Rising to go, Amelia had gazed at him proudly. "Sure do
look like my milk agrees with him." She had been doing
only light work till her baby was four months old. Then
she'd leave him with the other babies at Aunt Becky's.

"He's sure happy." Hildy had said, smiling. "Belly's
round as a drum. Come back when you hear the dinner
gong. He'll need his milk every two or three hours."

"When the wet-nurse comes. . . ."

"I'm going to tell Master Richard to send someone to
catch up with his messenger and say we don't need a
woman. Her milk might not suit him or her nipple
mightn't."

Those had been the reasons she had given Master
Richard as she held the bright head against her shoulder.
They had been true enough. But the deep, main reason had
been that Richie had become her baby. He still was.

This day, Amelia was collecting the rest of the laundry as
Hildy stripped Miss Lou's bed—much too big now—while
her mistress sat in the rocker, dutifully sipping the honey-
sweetened tea of St. John's wort and ginseng that Aunt
Becky prescribed for spells of the blues. This wasn't a spell
of Miss Lou's. She didn't eat much more than she slept.
Hildy, from her little room next door, waked through the
night to hear her walking up and down, up and down, like
someone soothing a cranky child. Only there was nothing in
her arms but sorrow.

As she put on sheets woven from flax grown, retted,
combed, and spun at the plantation, Hildy talked briskly,

trying to win more from Miss Lou than a listless nod or: "Do what you judge best, Hildy."

"The smokehouses are plumb full of hams and bacon. We finished making sausage yesterday, and there's plenty of lard, enough extra that, if we put some butter with it, we can trade it at the store for coffee and white sugar, and there's several barrels of sorghum molasses to swap, too. The corn's all cribbed, and a load taken to the mill. Aunt Becky and the girls who help tend the children are shelling out the dried beans and peas, and the root cellars are filling up with potatoes and turnips and cabbages. The older children are hunting nuts and persimmons. We'll eat good this winter, Miss Lou."

Waverly people always did. They could help themselves to the milk kept cool in the springhouse, even churn butter if they'd a mind to. For extra meat, men hunted 'coons, 'possums, and squirrels. Anyone who chose to could keep chickens and have their own garden patch. The same good smells filled the cabins and the big house: Tom-fuller, hickory nut grot, Tom-budha, and roasting ears, potatoes, ashcakes, and pound cakes baking in the ashes.

Miss Lou set her cup down with a sharpness that made Hildy straighten and turn to her. Those eyes, the color of blue flax flowers, were sunk in dark hollows! Hildy's heart constricted. Never robust, this beloved woman looked so frail and brittle that it was a wonder her bones didn't snap. There was no luster to the once beautiful wheat-yellow hair she hadn't yet combed this morning, and a faintly sour smell came from her nightgown—Miss Lou, who used to be so dainty!

"Hildy," Miss Lou whispered. "I don't know what to do."

Never had Hildy heard those words from a white person.

Maybe what they planned to do was wrong but they were sure about it. It was as if the solid oak floor rolled and buckled beneath her feet. She swallowed to get control of her voice. "How . . . how do you mean, Miss Lou?"

"You remember Chief Ross and his wife came calling last week on their way to Tahlequah?"

Hildy did, of course. How could she forget that fancy carriage with the little black boy in uniform perched up behind? The second Mrs. Ross, a Quaker lady from Delaware, was pleasant and gentle-spoken, but Hildy had had a feeling she'd never feel at home in what must seem to her the edge of the world.

The chief, a short, dignified man with red hair faded by his seventy-two years, was only an eighth Cherokee, but, although he owned 100 slaves and lived in a colonnaded mansion reached by a rose-bordered drive half a mile long, he had the trust and support of the mostly poor full-bloods and "pin" Indians who wore crossed pins on their coats to show they were converts of Northern missionaries who preached Abolition along with Jesus.

Ross's Cherokee wife had died on the horrible Trail of Tears over which, in 1838, the Cherokees had made their forced journey from the East to Indian Territory. They had buried 4,000 of their people along the way. Also driven from their ancestral Eastern homes were the Chickasaws, Creeks, and Choctaws. The Seminoles in the Florida swamps put up a long and desperate fight, but at last they came, too—all that could be caught.

There had been treaties, to be sure. The government liked its robberies legal, Master Richard used to say. The master's parents had died on the way West, although like most wealthy mixed-bloods they'd traveled pretty comfortably by steamboat and wagon, along with their slaves. He'd

14

been raised by the aunt and uncle who had built Waverly into a plantation almost as prosperous as the one by the same name in Georgia that they'd been forced to sell for next to nothing. The aunt and uncle were childless except for two daughters the uncle had by a pretty quadroon who had died on the Trail.

Fortunately for Master Richard's uncle, he hadn't been a signer of the treaty which violated tribal law. The signers, well-to-do mixed-bloods, believed removal was inevitable and the only way the Cherokees could live unmolested by the whites, but to the majority of full-bloods they were traitors. Master Richard had said they were condemned to death by their clansmen, who drew lots for the part of executioners. Before dawn on a June morning twenty-two years ago, John Ridge had been stabbed to death by twenty-five men in front of his horrified wife. At the same hour, his cousin, Elias Boudinot, had been killed and slashed with tomahawks. Later that day, Major Ridge, John's father, had been shot and killed from ambush.

The only signer to escape had been Stand Watie, Boudinot's brother, who had been warned by a friend. In spite of the danger, Watie had ridden to Boudinot's home and uncovered the mutilated body. They were full brothers, although out of respect for a white man who'd befriended Stand while he was getting a higher education in Connecticut, he had taken his name. Turning to the crowd that surely included conspirators, Watie had offered $10,000 to anyone who'd tell him who had hacked his brother's face.

No one had spoken. No one had attacked him. He rode away, the only signer of the treaty to live. There were killings back and forth for years, including the murder of Watie's younger brother, but in spite of the bitterness on both sides the Cherokees prospered in their new country. The tribe set up schools, and there were two newspapers. Master Richard had been a member of the Masonic Lodge in Tahlequah. Miss Alice attended the Female Seminary there, and Master Edmund, graduated from the one for boys, went East to medical school, where he was still studying. Miss Alice had married a friend Edmund had brought home for a visit and lived now in Boston, a shame when her mama needed her so badly.

Chief Ross had claimed innocence in the treaty signers' deaths, but from then on Watie had been his implacable enemy—and Watie, leader of most of the mixed-blood slave owners, was now raising men to fight for the Confederacy.

These griefs and murders flashed through Hildy's mind. She poured more tea for her mistress. "Did Chief Ross say something to fret you, Miss Lou?"

"He's fretted himself, poor soul." Miss Lou smiled faintly. "As you know, he's favored the Union . . . which happens to still owe the Cherokees five million dollars for our lands in the East. He's done his best to stay neutral, although General Ben McCulloch tried to persuade him to join the South. So has the Indian Commissioner, Albert Pike, with his wagonloads of presents."

Hildy nodded, chuckling at the memory of the immense bewhiskered man with his flowing hair who had passed by Waverly on his way to visit Ross. "Reckon he's trying to get the other tribes to go Confederate with his bolts of calico, store clothes, and trinkets."

"He's had good luck," Miss Lou said. "The Choctaw and Chickasaw Nations joined the Confederacy. The Creeks and Seminoles are split. After the Federals were beaten at Wilson's Creek . . . which left the Confederates in control of everything around us except Kansas to the north . . . Chief Ross was afraid Watie would overthrow him unless Ross let the Cherokees vote on whether or not to go with the South. He held a council late in August. As you know, most of the tribesmen there voted to make a treaty with the South and raise a regiment to serve under McCulloch."

Puzzled, Hildy nodded. That had happened a few days before they had learned about Master Richard's death. "Yes, Miss Lou, and Stand Watie, he's heading up his own Cherokee mounted volunteers."

"Yes, but plenty of Cherokees favor the Union. A great many Creeks do, too. Like the Cherokees, they have a feud going back to when their mixed-blood chief, William McIntosh, signed the removal treaty. He was killed for treason, but his sons survived. They can fight for the South and get revenge on the full-bloods who are mostly for the Union."

Miss Lou paused as if her strength had given out. She shivered although the room was comfortable. Hildy put a shawl around her and built up the fire.

"Whatever the rest of this is, Miss Lou, it can wait till you've had your breakfast. Could you relish some milk toast?"

Miss Lou raised a silencing hand. "Chief Ross thinks there's going to be nothing but trouble in Indian Territory till the war's over. All the Nations have blood feuds because of the removals, and now there'll be no outside force, like the Union Army, to keep any sort of peace."

Hildy couldn't get too worked up over the Trail of Tears although her mother and father had traveled it along with the Frazers' other slaves. They hadn't lived to tell her stories, but Aunt Becky, when spiteful, called her a "bone-wicked Coromantee" because her father's parents, captured as children on the Gold Coast, belonged to that fierce people. She doubted the Trail had been worse than crossing the ocean packed in the belly of a slave ship.

"Chief Ross," said Miss Lou, "advises me to move to Fort Smith. Opothleyaholo, the Creek chief, is for the Union, though he owns dozens of slaves. Chief Ross says that about four thousand Union Creeks, at least a thousand of them warriors, have gathered at Opothleyaholo's plantation and are moving north. Daniel McIntosh, an ordained Baptist minister, is after them with his First Creek Regiment, and then there's the Choctaw-Chickasaw regiment, a battalion of Creeks and Seminoles, and the Fourth Texas Cavalry."

"Lord have mercy!"

"Indeed. Ross hears Kansas jayhawkers have come down to help Opothleyaholo . . . what a name! He's eighty years old and still believes in his ancient gods. He's moving along the border of Cherokee lands, but hasn't crossed into them."

"Maybe all he wants is to get his people safe to Kansas."

"The McIntoshes will stop him if they can. It was his followers who murdered their father for signing a removal treaty back in Georgia." Miss Lou pushed distractedly at her tangled hair. "Chief Ross says rascals on both sides are using the war for an excuse to loot and kill."

"But if we go to Fort Smith. . . ."

"The chief has a trustworthy friend who's willing to take charge of Waverly for a share of the crops and increase of livestock."

Including slaves? Hildy thought to herself.

Miss Lou looked at Hildy in appeal. "If we go, I might lose the plantation for Richie. But if we stay, we could lose our lives."

"It's a hard choice, Miss Lou," Hildy said while thinking: *But at least you've got a choice. Slaves don't. Of*

course, *since we're valuable property, no one's likely to kill us.*
"Let me bring your breakfast and get some women started
on the washing. Then I'll brush your hair and we can talk
about all this, and pray."

Miss Lou's hand caught at hers, white and fragile against
Hildy's strong brown one. "I don't know what I'd do
without you, Hildy." She gave a tremulous laugh. "The best
thing I ever did for myself was taking you to raise."

*And the worst was letting Master Richard sell Justus . . .
though I guess you couldn't stop him.* A sudden thrill shot
through Hildy. *The war . . . all this upheaval . . . will it
somehow make it so Justus can come for me?*

Her heart raced at the thought, but, as she told Miss Lou
she'd be right back and left the room, the brief flare of hope
wavered and faded. Even if Justus were alive, even if he
came, how could she leave Miss Lou in her trouble? And
Richie, dear to her as a blood child? She grasped at the only
straw she could imagine. *Maybe . . . maybe Justus would stay
and help take care of Miss Lou.* That seemed so unlikely that
Hildy floundered into an even wilder fancy. *Maybe Miss Lou
would come North with us, where we'd be free but could still look
after her and Richie.*

Hildy dusted a bit of cinnamon on the milk toast, stirred
a tablespoon of molasses into a glass of milk, whipped
cream into some persimmon pudding, and sprinkled pecan
halves over it. Miss Lou needed all the nourishment she
could be coaxed to take, so Hildy used the best china and a
silver tray.

Once she had Miss Lou eating, Hildy went down the
back steps with the willow laundry basket. Cedar smoke
wafted up to tease her nostrils from the wash fires at the
creek. The ring of axes resounded from the timber beyond
the fields and orchards.

Most of the men were getting in the winter's wood for the cabins and the big house. Others plowed under stubble in the broad fields. Their exhortations to the mules mingled with the battling of the oak paddles on the white things that had been rubbed with soft soap and boiled in the big black kettle before they were spread on the bench to have stains beaten out of them.

Ruby and Jane, Justus's older sisters, like him tall, well-built, and the color of creamed coffee, joked as they wielded the paddles. Olive and Nell, tawny of skin, eyes, and hair, were actually Master Richard's cousins, daughters of his uncle and the quadroon who'd died on the Trail. The handsome sisters added Hildy's basketful to the clothes they were soaping.

All these women worked in the big house. Ruby's husband had been Tack, Master Richard's body servant, who had died trying to carry his dying master from the field. Marsh, Jane's husband and Master Edmund's servant, was off with him in Boston. Nell was married to the foreman, Harvey, and Olive to Jabez, a fine tailor who used to make his master's clothes and still did Master Edmund's. Their children, of varying ages and hues, clambered with Master Richie on the big, gray rocks along the creek. Younger children played in and out of Aunt Becky's double cabin where she and her girl helpers also looked after several old folks who had no families.

To Hildy's prideful eyes, Richie shone like a gold piece. She knew his sweet, fluting voice from all the others—her lamb, her own lamb. As soon as she helped Miss Lou dress, Hildy would bring Richie up to see his mama.

Miss Lou had drunk the milk, eaten a little of the pudding and toast, and was putting on one of the dyed black gowns that made her look so pale. Hildy buttoned the dress, and, while she brushed the light brown hair, once silky but now dry and lifeless, she told Miss Lou about the work going on outside. Miss Lou showed no flicker of interest. It was a good thing Harvey was honest and smart and kept things going without a master to answer to.

Hildy made as graceful a twist as she could of the limp hair and secured it with pins and jet combs. "Miss Lou," she ventured, "maybe you should ask Master Edmund to come home. He's up there with all those Yankees, and. . . ."

"I won't interrupt his studies." From the firmness of Miss Lou's tone, these days usually vague and hesitant, Hildy knew she had already struggled with this. "With mail so uncertain, I sent Edmund three letters about his father. I won't try to stop him if he decides he has to volunteer for the Army. I've assured him we're managing quite well at Waverly, thanks to our black family, and he need have no concern about us."

"But, Miss Lou! If Chief Ross thinks you'd better leave. . . ."

"I'm praying over it." Miss Lou closed her eyes. "Hildy, it was wrong for Master Richard to part you and Justus. My lawyer is drawing up papers to free you both."

"Free me?" Hildy felt as if gongs echoed in her head.

"Yes. If . . ."—the soft voice faltered but went on—"if you want to try to find Justus, I'll give you enough cash money for the journey and to keep you till you find employment."

Hildy felt as if her head was full of air and about to float away. "Oh, Miss Lou!"

"It's only right. The way I miss my husband makes me know what a terrible thing we did in separating you. I begged Richard, but perhaps I could have done more."

"Don't see what." Hildy had a sudden illuminating

thought. "Why, Miss Lou, bless your heart! When you stop to think about it, white ladies with mean husbands are almost as bad off as slaves."

"Master Richard was never mean to me, but. . . ."

"I know," comforted Hildy. "When he got sot, he was sot for sure."

Her mind churned. How would she find Justus? Many runaways kept going till they were safe across the Canadian border. Hildy had never been off the plantation except for trips to Tahlequah a few times. There were some bad people out in the world beyond Waverly, some who'd destroy your free papers and keep you for a slave or sell you. Still, she had to take this chance. "I'll go, Miss Lou . . . and, if the good God lets me find Justus, we'll come back and help you. Just now, though, I'll fetch Richie to see you."

Passing down the hall past the dining room, Hildy heard the *clink* of silver. What could possess any of the women to polish silver on washday? She opened the door and froze.

Three men, in filthy buckskin and homespun, stuffed silver from the sideboard and cupboard into bags, including the huge claw-footed eggnog bowl, candelabra, and trays and pitchers of every size. Through the window, she saw horsemen gallop through Miss Lou's flowers. Down by the smokehouses, men loaded a wagon with meat. She saw all this in a flash.

The thieves laughed. One put down a shining pitcher and started for her. "Looky here, boys! Did you ever clap eyes on a purtier nigger wench?"

"That's not all we'll clap on her."

They stank of whiskey, tobacco, stale sweat. One looked Indian. *Richie! Miss Lou! Oh, God.* . . . Hildy glanced around for a weapon. She didn't scream because she prayed for a miracle—that Miss Lou, at the back of the house, wouldn't hear, that this trash would finish their stealing and leave. If only she could reach the fireplace and the poker. . . . She edged in that direction while the robbers came around the great table to advance on her.

"Hold off a minute, boys!" A whiskery beanpole who smelled rank as a boar hog came out of Master Richard's adjoining study with a bulging sack. "Bein' a pet house nigger, this 'n' likely knows where the money's kept."

Hildy lunged for the poker. He was on her like a panther, stench so foul it made her gag. "Where's massa keep his gold coin, gal?" Only snags remained of rotting teeth. One hand closed on her breast, fingernails digging.

With all her strength, Hildy jerked free and grabbed the poker. *What is going on outside? Where are the hands?* "There's no gold," she lied. "Master lost it all on slow horses he thought were fast."

"You might recollect better if we heat that poker and decorate you." The lanky man grinned. He seemed to be the leader of this gang who seemed to be plain thieves, not any kind of soldiers. "Tell us nice . . . treat us nice . . . and we might even leave you a dollar."

They had pistols and wicked knives, but they didn't want to kill her. Not yet. Apart from galloping horses, it hadn't been noisy outside, but suddenly firearms roared. Shrieks and howls reverberated.

What is going on out there? Have the robbers started fighting each other over the loot? Miss Lou had to hear.

Ignoring the uproar, the four marauders sidled toward Hildy. They could rush her, but the first one would get the poker across his face. With luck, she'd break one of their ugly jaws, splinter some teeth.

There was the *click* of a hammer thumbed back. Miss

Lou stood in the door, holding with both hands the heavy Remington .44 revolver Master Richard had taught her to load and shoot before he went to war. She shot the leader through the middle. "Hit them there and they'll die sometime," Master Richard had instructed.

Hildy crashed the poker down on the closest thief's head. He toppled, but didn't thrash around, yelling, like the gut-shot one. The two remaining had their guns out. Miss Lou blasted one in the face. The other shot her as Hildy swung the poker as hard as she could against the side of his neck.

She heard it snap. Above that sound came firing and yells, a thunder of hoofs, but although Hildy heard, it meant nothing, nor did the groaning curses of the dying looters. She fell on her knees by Miss Lou. Blood pumped from the wound, soaking the black cloth of the bodice.

A linen tablecloth protruded from a robber's bag. Hildy seized it, tore open Miss Lou's bodice and chemise, and stuffed the cloth over the ragged blood-pulsing hole.

"Richie!" gasped Miss Lou. Pink froth bubbled from her mouth. The fingers that had fired the revolver reached blindly and fell. She made a kind of choking noise.

"Miss Lou!" Hildy raised her. "Miss Lou, honey!"

The hazel eyes stared, but they weren't seeing anything. Hildy heard feet pounding up the hall. She saw blue legs, fringed buckskins, and plain old butternut homespuns. Lifting her gaze, she saw Justus. *Is he real?*

He shot the tall thief in the head, thumbed back the hammer, and finished off the one with the ruined face. A man in buckskin, accompanying Justus, bent to slice his knife across the throat of the robber she'd stunned with the poker.

Justus dropped to his knees beside her, felt for a pulse at

the side of Miss Lou's throat. He shook his head, shook it again as he saw the revolver by her hand. "Miss Lou used that?"

"She . . . she kept them off me. . . ." She stared at one of the dead robbers. "Are you with them?" she asked Justus.

"No, they're just a bunch of no-goods. Where's Master Richard?"

"Dead at Wilson's Creek." *Am I dreaming? Is Justus here? Is Miss Lou dead?* "Master Edmund's studying up in Boston."

Justus took in a sighing breath. He gripped Hildy's hand. "Miss Lou was a good lady. We'll bury her before we leave."

"Leave?"

"Well, sure!" His eyes caught hers. She breathed in the special scent of him. Yearning throbbed between them. "I've come back for you, Hildy. Joined the Army at Fort Scott and volunteered to join one of the detachments that are scouting this north part of the territory to keep Confederate troops from stopping the Union Creeks get safe over the border into Kansas."

Union soldiers? But . . . they aren't acting much different from the out-and-out bandits! Why did part of this dream come true have to be a nightmare?

As if he knew she couldn't think, Justus squeezed her fingers. "Get a quilt, sweetheart."

The buckskin-clad man with Justus stank almost as badly as the thieves. He peered into one of the sacks and chortled: "Look at these candlesticks and pitchers! All bagged and ready to go!"

Hildy scrambled up, started for him. "You can't . . . !"

Justus caught her wrist, gave her a warning look. His companion tied the bag and started out, saying: "Keep your

gal in line, Jus. She oughta be glad we're settin' her free."
He looked Hildy up and down. "Where's your master's
gold?"

"In other men's pockets." Hildy was amazed at how
easily she invented another lie. "He liked cards too much."

"You sure about that?"

Hildy looked him in the pale eyes. "Sure as sure."

"That's the gospel truth," said Justus. He gave her a
little shove. "Hurry and get that quilt."

These might be Union men, but it looked like to them
Justus was still a nigger. Hildy wasn't daft enough to get
him killed over the family silver. "I have to go see if Master
Richie's safe."

"I'll go with you," Justus said. "I've got to see my mama
and sisters."

He steered her past a number of dead men on the way to
the cabins. Except for one bearded man with a blue uniform
and a hole in his forehead, it was hard to tell to which band
the dead belonged—the thieves or the men with Justus.
They had one thing in common. They were all dead, some
with slit throats or bashed-in heads. Neither side was taking
prisoners or letting the wounded crawl away.

The big iron kettle spilled soapy linens that were being
trampled into the sodden earth. The kettle was too hot to
handle, but men were dousing it with rinse water from the
tubs. Some had taken over where the other gang had left
off, heaping wagons with corn from the cribs, all the cured
meat, butter, and cheese from the springhouse, and kegs of
molasses.

"Don't look, Hildy." Justus gripped her arm and drew
her along toward his mother's place. The wails of frightened children came from behind the barred door. "Mama,
it's me!" Justus pounded on the heavy oak boards.

The door opened in a twinkling. Aunt Becky stared up at her tall son. The wrinkles of her brown skin seemed to smooth, and her eyes shone. "My Lord, dear God!" She lifted trembling hands to touch his face. "Oh, child! Haven't I prayed . . . every night and day I've prayed . . . to lay eyes on you again?"

They held each other closely, Justus's cheeks as wet as his mother's and sisters' who swarmed to hug him.

"You're real!" Jane laughed as she wept.

Aunt Becky turned to jerk her head toward the rambunctious foragers. "Why you with that white trash, boy?"

"They're mostly jayhawkers, all legal now, rigged out in uniforms"—Justus shrugged—"but I'd have ridden with Old Nick himself to get home."

Small heads began to pop up from behind cots and the chest. Half-grown girls scuttled in from the other cabin with their charges. Master Richie ran to Hildy and buried his face in her lap.

"We . . . we heard the guns, Hildy! I want Mama!"

How to tell him? Should he see her? Poor lamb, no Mama now, or Daddy. . . . Master Edmund and Miss Alice both back East. . . . Thoughts spinning crazily as a broken mill wheel, unable to speak even if she knew what to say, Hildy hugged the little boy.

Harvey, the tall foreman, and Jabez, the mulatto tailor, rushed in with a mallet and sickle they'd snatched up for weapons. "Bless God, you're all right!" Harvey gasped to his wife Nell as Jabez hugged Olive. They recognized Justus in the same moment.

"Where'd you get that blue coat and a gun, Jus?" demanded Harvey. "You with this gang of thievin' rascals?"

"That thievin' bunch wouldn't have left a solitary egg, let alone a chicken!" Justus gave a short laugh. "Fact is,

27

Harve, if we hadn't turned up, more'n likely all of you'd get hustled off to be sold in Fort Smith." Justus raised his voice to reach the others who came crowding in. "We're Union men. No one'll hurt you, long as you don't get in their way. Miss Lou's dead. . . ."

Wails broke out. Justus held up his hand. "The bandits did it, not us! She'll be buried decent."

"Master Richard, he's dead, too," mumbled Harvey. "What we goin' to do? Oh, Lordy, what we goin' to do?"

"You want to be Lincoln soldiers?" Justus asked.

"Soldiers?" Harvey and Jabez shrank, but some of the younger men whooped and yelled. "Soldiers? Us?"

"General Jim Lane'll take you," Justus explained. "Mark my words, it won't be too long till there's goin' to be whole regiments of black men!"

"Fighting the masters?" Jabez choked. "Sweet Lord Jesus! If they caught us, they'd skin us alive!"

"They'll shoot us if they can, that's certain."

Justus sounded so cheerfully confident that Hildy's heart swelled with pride, even in her grief. He'd always been the man she loved, but now he wasn't anybody's slave! He was a warrior, just like those wild Indians farther West. Now he grinned at his old friends, and held up his revolver. A black man with a gun!

"If you want to join the Army, hurry and get ready to come with us. We're down here to help Union Creeks fight off that whole damn boilin' of Confederate Creeks, Chicka-saws, Seminoles, and Cherokees . . . even Texans!"

"You aim to fight with all that plunder in the wagons?" asked Harvey.

"Call it our supply train." Justus laughed, then sobered. "You women and whatever men don't want to be soldiers, you got two choices. Stay here and hide out when one side or the other tears through, or head for Kansas with all you can carry. You'll be free there. No one'll send you back or sell you."

His mother caught his arms. "Lord God, boy, I've lived here my whole born days! I don't know nothin' about Kansas 'cept it's full and runnin' over with crazy folks."

Harvey pondered, turned to his gold-skinned wife, Nell, Master Richard's cousin. She looked at him above the coppery hair of their three light-skinned children. "Let's go, Harvey, for the children's sake," she pleaded. "If we stay and the South wins, we be slaves for always."

After a second's hesitation, he threw back his head. "We'll go," he said.

"So will we!" echoed a score of others.

"Then fill up the carriage and carts and anything that'll hold stuff," Justus advised. "No use leavin' things for the next raiders. Take any mules and cows the soldiers leave. Everything at Waverly came from your sweat."

Jabez caught Harvey's arm. "Don't be taking everything! Some of us druther stay . . . build cabins way back in the woods."

Olive, his tawny-haired wife, nodded. "Sounds better to me than trying to get North. S'posin' you meet up with more bushwhackers or Confederates than you can fight off? You'll get sold if they don't kill you."

Harvey's shoulders hunched forward but his tone was stubborn. "You that feels like that, come along, and we'll share out whatever the soldiers leave."

"I'm stayin'!" Aunt Becky appealed to her tall, handsome daughters. "Ruby! Jane! Don't be leavin' your old mama, at least not the both of you!"

"I got to stay, Mama." Jane put an arm around the frightened old woman. "Marsh wouldn't know where else to look when he and Master Edmund come back."

"My man died tryin' to haul Master Richard out of the firing," Ruby said. "I love you, Mama, but I'm takin' my children up where they'll never be sold." She added in a wondering tone: "Where they be free! Free! Can't wrap my mind around that yet."

"You'll get used to it," Justus assured her.

"Why can't we follow along with you?" Ruby asked.

"Too dangerous. There's bound to be fighting. On top of that, we can't be slowed down. You go with Harve's bunch, honey." He gave his sister a gentle push. "Go get your things."

She hurried off with the others. At last Justus caught Hildy to him, tight as he could with Master Richie in between, and kissed her long and hard and sweet. Oh, so sweet. . . .

"Thought my heart would break with longin' for you," he whispered. "All the time I was helpin' runaways go North, I tried to figger how to get you loose 'thout gettin' caught my ownself. When the war broke out, I was in Canada . . . come down and drove supply wagons for an Ohio regiment till I heard about Lane's jayhawkers bringin' out slaves from Missouri. Why not Indian Territory? I say to myself. Barely got sworn in at Fort Scott when word came that a lot of Union Creeks, headin' for Kansas, was being chased by all manner of Secesh. When Colonel Jennison called for volunteers to help the Union Creeks, you bet I was first in line."

"Oh, if you could just have got here before Miss Lou. . . ."

His tone hardened a little. "Well, at least you don't have to feel bad about leavin' her. Anything you need, get it fast, sugar. I'll find you a horse or mule."

She blinked. "You . . . want I should come with you?"

"Why else you reckon I'm here?"

"But . . . how'll I bring Master Richie?"

"You can't. And, Hildy, he's not Master Richie. You never goin' to call anyone master again!"

"I can't leave him."

"Sure you can! My mama and sis'll look after him, or someone can take him to Chief Ross's place."

Richie wailed and gripped her around the knees. Hildy knelt to hold him.

"Leave him," Justus ordered.

"I've looked after him since the hour he was born."

"Yes, instead of you and me havin' a child. A leech, that's what he is, a little white leech!" Justus's hands closed on Richie as if to force him away.

Hildy shielded the boy with her body. "You go on with your soldiers. I'll travel with Harvey and the others."

"You daft, woman?"

"Why?"

"What's goin' to happen if Secesh catch a bunch of run-aways with a little white brat?"

He was right. Richie's presence could make the difference between being saved alive and sold, or death by flogging or burning. She couldn't put such danger on the rest. Although her heart chilled, she said: "I'll go North with him alone, then."

"You're crazy!" Justus's voice dropped, filled with hurt and pain that stabbed her deeply. "I'm your own married husband. Don't that matter?"

"I love you! I do, Justus!" She kept her arms around the boy. "But. . . ."

"That bleached-out little maggot couldn't suck milk out of you, but he sure sucked out who you are!" Justus's powerful hands flexed, hands she loved but that could snap

31

Richie's neck like a dry twig.

Hildy backed away with the child. Justus gave a laugh that was close to a sob before he swallowed. "Go alone, you're better off without a mule or horse. Won't be so easy seen or tracked, and you won't get killed by some thief. I remember you can wear Miss Lou's shoes. Better find a couple of stout pairs . . . and warm clothes. It's a long walk to Kansas."

Tears filled Hildy's eyes. She tried to speak, couldn't, and mutely stretched out her hand. To see him just these few minutes, then maybe never again! It was too hard, too hard!

"You can pick up the Military Road to Fort Scott, if you follow the creek east about five miles," Justus told her. "Fade into the timber when you hear anyone comin', but try not to get too far from it."

A bugle sounded. "Best place for you to go is to some Quaker folks named Parks, who run a mill close to Trading Post," Justus decided. "They be friends of the Wares, those folks who helped me get away. I'd send you to them, if they didn't live across the Missouri line where you could be picked up for a runaway. The girl, Christy, she'd be a good friend to you. If you meet her and her folks, tell them I pray for them every day of this world."

The bugle called again. Hildy couldn't bear to let him go, clung to him when he kissed her. He had to loosen her hands away. "After the war," he promised. "After the war, I'll find you sure!" He hurried off.

Hildy went light-headed and dizzy as if tight bands holding her skull together were slashed. But this was no time for fainting. "Richie," she said. "We have to go, you and me, honey boy."

"Mama go, too?"

"Your mama. . . ." Hildy couldn't keep from sobbin That frightened Richie. He tugged at her.

"I want Mama!"

"Honey, you have to tell her good bye. Like you did you daddy. . . ."

"Daddy's dead! He was a brave, brave so'jer!"

"So was your mama, Richie. Just as brave as your daddy. . . ."

"Gracious' sake, Hildy!" Aunt Becky summoned her daughters with a jerk of her head. "Come along, Master Richie. Your mama's gone to be with Jesus. You kiss her and I'll cut off a piece of her hair for you."

The disappearing soldiers had dug the grave. One blue-coated man waited by it and the quilt-wrapped body. "I'm a minister of the United Brethren," he said. "I'll give a service for the lady."

Even the Waverly men who planned to join the soldiers gathered for the brief ceremony, but it was the women who lowered Miss Lou into the grave. Frost had killed the flowers she loved so much, but Harvey and Jabez broke off cedar limbs to put over her and soften the fall of the red earth.

Then, over the grave of their mistress, the folk of Waverly wished each other luck and gave Richie a kiss or pat on the head before those who wanted to join the Army went off after them and Jabez's and Harvey's groups hurried to finish their preparations.

"Where . . . where we going, Hildy?" Richie wasn't letting go of her for an instant. He hadn't wanted to kiss his mother, but he held tightly to the lock of hair Aunt Becky had put in a little tin box for him.

"We're goin' where bad men won't be ridin' through."

"Can . . . can I take my toys?"

"Just a few, darlin'. We have to carry food and blankets and some clothes. You be brave now and help me."

How long would it be before one rampaging bunch or another burned the house after looting whatever the robbers and soldiers had left? She hoped Harvey's and Jabez's bands took a lot of useful things. Nell and Olive had vowed to rescue what they could of family heirlooms and hide them in the woods till Master Edmund or Miss Alice came for them.

"Go to your room, Richie," Hildy said. "Get out three sets of clothes . . . don't forget your socks and drawers! Bring your other shoes, your mittens and wool cap, and a jacket. . . ."

"It's not cold. . . ."

"It will be."

"Can I bring my little men?" He meant his lead soldiers. Hadn't he seen soldiers enough for the rest of his life? But they had been his last birthday gift from his father and were his favorite toys.

"Pick the eight you like best."

"What . . . what'll happen to the rest?"

"Ruby and Jane and Olive will likely hide them away with your other things." *Though if you ever set eyes on them again,* she thought to herself, *you'll likely be too old to play with them.*

His mouth quivered. "I can't go to sleep without Mister Bun."

Knitted from softest blue wool by Miss Lou and stuffed with cotton lint, the flop-eared bunny had been mended till probably no original stitch remained, but, however bold and venturesome Richie was by day, at bedtime he wanted the comfort of his grimy old companion.

"Of course, we'll take Mister Bun."

"Do . . . do we got to go today?"

"As quick as ever we can, child."

He ran to his room like a scared little shadow. Hildy felt like a thief when she got out Miss Lou's sturdiest shoes, but she knew bruising and cutting her feet would slow down their journey. Miss Lou's lined, wool, hooded cape would keep Hildy warm by day and serve as a blanket by night. Although no one had bothered anything else in the room, likely out of respect for a woman who'd died defending her slave, they had cleaned out the crystal bowl where Miss Lou kept a little silver and gold. Most of Waverly's money was invested with trading enterprises.

Hildy took a last look around Miss Lou's room, full of the scent and memories of the woman who had raised her. *Good bye, Miss Lou. Good bye, my sweet lady. . . . I'll do my best for Richie, but I'm afraid, and Justus's gone and . . . and if you can at all, Miss Lou, help me!*

Hildy closed the door and stumbled blindly into her own room. One blanket was all she could carry. She laughed shakily to realize she had her own Mr. Bun, the indigo, wool blanket Miss Lou had woven with her own hands and given her one Christmas. Hildy spread it on the bed, put on it a change of clothes for herself and the shoes, thread, scissors, and needles, then carried the blanket to the kitchen to add a skillet, cook pot, forks and spoons, bacon, venison jerky, beans, hominy, cornmeal, salt, coffee, dried peaches, apples, and pears. They'd be like candy to Richie, but food as well. She got flint and steel, and then remembered Master Richard's box of matches in the study by his chest of Havana cigars. They'd be handy when a fire was needed in a hurry.

The robust odor of the tobacco made her glance around

as if Master Richard might stroll into the carpeted, velvet-draped room. She hoped, somehow, the books, footed globe, rosewood furniture, and bronze figures would survive to belong to Master Edmund or Richie, although God only knew what would happen to any of them, much less to things.

Going to Richie's room, she helped him pack Mr. Bun, his little men, and clothing in a pillowcase he could carry, and added the rest to her burden.

So much here they needed, but there was no use starting out with more than they could carry. *The butcher knife . . . useful, and a weapon.* She wrapped the blade with a dish towel and thrust it through an improvised sash made of two towels tied together.

Through the window, she saw the trees bounded by their shadows the way it was at noon. *Had the world ended in just one morning? Miss Lou, Miss Lou, good bye.*

Hildy took Richie's hand and a deep breath. "Come on, honey boy. Tell Mister Bun we're going where there won't be all this trouble." She had a good mind to try to find that Christy Ware that Justus had mentioned, the one who'd helped him get away North. But the first safe place she found for Richie, that's where they'd stay till this was all over.

"My little men'll help us," Richie said. "They're so'jers just like Daddy."

Which got him and Tack buried up there at Wilson's Creek in Missouri.

"Will we ever come back?" the child asked.

"Most likely you will, Richie," she comforted. "After the war. After Master Edmund comes home."

But I won't. Never.

CHAPTER TWO

Ellen Ware, her two daughters, Christy and Beth, Sarah Morrow, and the survivors of the burning of Rose Haven, made their heavily laden way, along with their animals, through the underground passage toward the secret valley that spread below the opening now blocked by a woman whose skin was as brown as her leather garments—a woman who wanted to know who they were and why they had come?

When the Wares had begun to fear they might need to hide from the thieves and the Confederate guerrillas who were raiding the homes of Union sympathizers along the turbulent border of Kansas and Missouri, Christy and her father had discovered this way to the valley. Little more than a week ago, guerrilla raiders had shot Jonathan Ware, dead, on his own threshold and killed most of the livestock. Ironically a wounded man, who was probably a guerrilla, lay recovering at this moment in the Ware house.

Jonathan Ware's family had found no refuge at Rose Haven, the grand plantation of the Jardines' whose daughter was the wife of Charlie Ware. Instead the Ware females and their friend, Sarah, had found ruins, a slaughtered Bishop Jardine, his wife Lavinia, already an invalid, demented by his death, and Melissa Jardine Ware near childbirth.

Lavinia Jardine, perhaps mercifully, died before her daughter was fit to travel. Her old nurse, Aunt Phronie, and Phronie's beautiful half white daughter Lilah had come with Melissa. Now, after their journey from the plantation, the remnants of two very different families, one of wealthy slave owners, one of a Universalist minister who had helped runaway slaves escape, gazed at this woman who barred their way.

Her tunic was pieced together from a number of small hides that had been patched often. Neither dress nor moccasins were ornamented or fringed. Not one of the incomers questioned the woman's authority, although any one of them, even Phronie, could have physically overwhelmed her. She was like the spirit of the valley made flesh. Beyond her, in the shadows, a pretty brown-skinned woman sat with her arms loosely clasping a white child with curly golden hair who looked about five. Beth saw him, too, and gave a bounce of excitement. When her mother didn't speak, Christy stepped forward.

"Perhaps you don't know there's a war outside. . . ."

"There's always a war." The old woman's English was very good, but had a soft Scot's burr. She nodded toward the dark young woman. "Hildy told me about this one. North and South. Union. Confederacy." She gave a lift of her shoulders. "Whichever side wins, they'll steal my people's land."

"Aren't you Osage?" asked Sarah. "I am."

Keen black eyes examined her. "You look like my dear friend, Si-zhe-Wah'i, Shy Deer, who the missionaries called Mary. She married a Frenchman, I recall. You have his eyes. It was a real wedding, according to our customs, not just going off into the bushes."

"Then you went to school at Harmony Mission with my mother?" cried Sarah between joy and disbelief.

"Yes. Like me, Shy Deer was the eldest daughter of an important family and had the sacred spider on both hands . . . see?" She held out the backs of her hands. Black spiders moved when she flexed her fingers. "I remember those," Sarah whispered. "I wanted to have them."

"I don't suppose you do now." The woman's tone was dry. "Shy Deer was of the Deer Clan and I of the Eagle. I hoped she would marry my brother, but once the Frenchman watched her with eyes like the sky . . . well, after all, the Deer clan are Sky People."

"Sky People?" Sarah repeated.

The woman frowned. "Shy Deer never taught you who you are?"

"She died of cholera when I was three. My father was sickening and took me to the mission before he died. That was after the Osages moved to Kansas."

Teeth the color of old ivory showed in the wrinkled face. "I didn't go."

Ellen Ware gasped. "You've lived here since . . . since Eighteen Thirty-Seven?"

"No. I was married to a man of Scotland, a freighter on the Santa Fé Trail. I used to travel with him, and cook. He died defending me from a teamster who thought, because I was Indian, I was for anyone's pleasure." She paused. "I had no wish to live on the Kansas reservation or marry again. The old ones of my people knew about this valley. They said some of the Land or War People lived here when the Sky or Peace People found them, and they united to become the Children of the Middle Waters, the Osage." She thought a moment as if calling back things no longer important. "It was while the whites were fighting the war with Mexico that I came here."

"Eighteen Forty-Six?" murmured Sarah. "That's still a long time."

"At first it was. Not now."

"No one's come here?"

39

"Just Hildy"—the Osage woman gestured to her side—"and the child. They've run from the white man's war. And winters ago, a hunter came once, after a bear. He shot at it right here. The bear escaped into the valley, but rocks fell on the hunter. His bones are still under them."

"Do animals find their way in very often?" asked an awed Beth.

"Bears. Sometimes a panther."

"I suppose you snare them for food and hides," Sarah ventured.

"No. Whatever enters the valley dies in its own time. Then I take the hides, even the meat if it isn't tainted. There is no killing here."

Sarah protested: "But Osages hunt!"

"The Wa-kon of this valley, its mystery power, gave me a vision. This is a place of life."

"The panthers must have killed to live!" objected Sarah.

The valley's guardian smiled. "That is their Wa-kon. I don't have to kill to live. Besides nuts and fruit and wild foods, I have two bee gums, and grow corn, squash, and pumpkins as my people always have." She seemed to make a decision. "I am One Eagle, but my husband called me Star."

"A lovely name," said Ellen Ware.

"It belongs to Sky People," admitted the woman. "But my husband Geordie said my eyes were like star shine in the night. Every day, all these years, I've talked with him . . . in his language, for he never could learn mine. Sometimes, now, I hear him answer." She glanced kindly at Melissa and Lilah who seemed dazed by all that had happened. "You are tired. Sit down. Now tell me who you are."

Since no one else spoke, Christy did. She introduced Sarah, Melissa, Lilah, and Phronie, then gave her own, her mother's, and her sister's names.

On hearing them, Hildy sprang up. "Ware? You be the Wares who helped my man, Justus?"

"Justus?" Startled, Christy stared at the other. "You're his wife . . . Hildy?"

"Yes. Married by the preacher and all, but that didn't matter when Master Richard. . . ." Glancing down at the little white child hanging to her skirt, Hildy didn't finish.

"We helped him get over to Kansas, where John Brown took him North," Christy said. "He wanted to save enough money to buy your freedom."

"Not enough money in the world to do that as long as Master Richard was alive." The soft voice was bitter and sad at the same time. "But Master Richard got himself killed at Wilson's Creek. Bandits killed Miss Lou. Then Justus came along with some Union soldiers, but I couldn't go with him. . . ."

"Justus is a soldier?" Christy burst out.

Hildy's smile was wry. "This bunch were down to help the Union Creeks fight off the Confederate ones, but they finished stealing what the bandits had started loading up."

"Trust the heavy eyebrows . . . the whites . . . to break the Indian nations in half." The leather-clad woman's voice was weary.

"Justus told me to ask for you at Parkses' mill," went on Hildy. "Richie and me got off the Military Road when we saw anyone coming, but we were too slow one day and this gang of cut-throats took after us. Ran us through the brush and timber till I nearly fell into a sinkhole hid by a spice-bush. We crawled down. Pesky varmints was yelling and tearing around. Reckon they never saw the sinkhole. Long way off, I saw light, so we started toward it, walking real careful. When we were far enough inside that I reckoned the devils couldn't notice, I lit a candle. We came out of that littlest cave on the far side, yonder."

"So Justus doesn't know where you are?"

"No. But he sent me to the Parkses, so, when this war's over, he'll come there . . . if he's alive."

Star sighed, keen eyes looking at each newcomer in turn. "You are welcome to the valley so long as you need refuge. Come, I'll show you several other caves that are easier for living." The valley's guardian grinned. "Caves that don't have a smashed hunter in them."

Lilah and Melissa waited in what they began to call the River Cave while Star showed the others the cave she thought best suited to them, a spacious limestone grotto. "It's close to the river"—she pointed out—"but high enough not to flood. There's this big chamber with a fairly level floor for cooking and work, and two shallow rooms for sleeping. We can wall up the front with rocks and mud mortar, make a fireplace and smoke hole. If you have a saw, you can make a door out of wood." Reading their faces, she explained: "It'll be dark, but a fire will give light. You could make a big door and leave it open when the weather's good. And in summer, you can knock out some of the rocks to let in fresh air and light." Her face lit up. "No! In summer, if you're still here, we'll build a long house of the kind my people live in, one big enough for everyone."

"Of logs?" Christy was dubious, remembering the raising of the Ware's happy house and how much skilled labor it had taken. Rather than try to saw logs to make a door, she and Sarah could bring back the door of one of the corncribs; there certainly wasn't any corn left to protect.

"We can build a house," Star assured her guests. "There are plenty of young hickories for poles and cat-tails and bark for walls and roof. I could have made a small round lodge of the kind my people used when hunting buffalo on the plains, but when I came here, it seemed good to dwell in Mother Earth as our people did in the beginning before the Sky folk came." She smiled at Sarah. "You are of the Sky People, daughter of my friend. Wah'-kon-tah has surely brought you here."

Sarah looked eagerly at the older woman. "I hope you'll tell me more about my parents and my people."

"Winter is a grand time for stories, my husband always said." Star laughed as she watched the fair-haired little boy grasp Beth's hand and tug her off to admire some secret of his. "How fine it is to see children again! You even have a baby, with another coming." For Lilah was heavy with child, quite probably by Melissa's careless, handsome brother who was off fighting for the South. As, to Christy's grief, was her brother, Charlie, who had married Melissa.

"Yes, and we'd better help Melissa and Lilah down here," Ellen said. "The cave's nice and dry. We can leave an overhang outside the wall where we can work on fine days."

"Like a porch," said Phronie, cheering a bit.

"There's two smaller caves across the valley, if you'd rather have separate dwellings."

"Right now," said Ellen, "I think we'd like to stay together."

With Hildy and Star helping, the supplies were carried to the cave. Star had a long band of leather that she slipped around bundles in order to carry them more easily. By placing the band where hair and forehead met and securing the chicken basket with the other end of the loop, she easily carried the scolding fowl down the hazardous rocks.

These and the other Jardine chickens were turned loose near a makeshift shelter of stripped branches closing all but an entry to a long shallow cave. The door could be closed with more branches at night till some kind of door was fashioned. A fallen tree with plenty of good roosting limbs had been dragged inside. Lilah and Melissa, still exhausted, were persuaded to rest on rush mats Star brought while the others unpacked and put things out of the way on numerous ledges. The willow chest, cleaned of chickens, held sheets and Melissa's baby's clothing. Strange that a cave might be the first home remembered by the child who would have been heir to Rose Haven!

Nooning sunlight shone almost to the back of the stone room, pleasantly warming it, but, in a few more hours, it would be shaded again. They stopped work to go to Star's home, sit out in the sun, and share herb-flavored stew of chopped hickory nuts, dried corn, and squash ladled with a wood spoon into wood bowls. The incomers contributed cold cornbread, butter, and buttermilk.

"I had forgotten how good butter tastes," Star allowed. "Many inventions of the heavy eyebrows are useful. My people traded with the French long before the Americans came, back when they were arguing with the Spaniards over who owned our country." She glanced at the iron kettle and an axe, hoe, and shovel leaning against the rock wall. "I brought as many good things as I could from the cabin where we lived when Geordie wasn't freighting, but I've never wanted anything, even salt, enough to leave the valley."

"My husband swapped molasses and corn for a year's supply of salt at the store in Trading Post," Ellen said. "We have dried red peppers, too, that are good seasoning. We'll share."

Star nodded as if that were only to be expected. "I have much dried fruit and nuts, besides my crops. There will be food enough for everyone." She got to her feet. "We'll begin the wall of your home this afternoon and finish it tomorrow. You're welcome to sleep in my cave, if you wish, but it should be warm enough here if you have a fire."

"Thank you." Ellen's face lightened as she watched her daughter-in-law nurse Charlie's son, Joely. "We'll stay here. I think we'll all want to sleep close together tonight anyway."

The good weather held, although it was cool next morning. By mid-afternoon, the mud-mortared rocks, mostly gray but also red, yellow, and white, walled in all but the door space of the cave. A rock chimney rising from above the fireplace jutted out to form part of the wall.

It was dark inside, but a warm, welcoming dark, scented with cedar and oak boughs burned last night. In the wreck of the world they'd known, in the midst of nightmare and disaster, what a blessing to find Star and Hildy in the valley! Beth, nearly two years older than Richie, took charge of him to their mutual enjoyment and their elders' relief.

"If we hurry," said Christy, shielding her eyes toward the sun, "we can bring the Wyandotte hens and all but one cow back before night."

"The cows can carry several mattresses," Ellen said. She rubbed her back. "Your rush mat helped a lot, Star, but I need a little more between me and the ground."

Beth caught Christy's hand. "Bring Robbie! Please!"

They hadn't brought the little border collie yesterday for fear he'd get under Melissa's or Lilah's uncertain feet, or, indeed, those of any of the burdened persons or animals he might have tripped. Christy looked at Star for permission.

"Robbie's a good dog, but he'll chase rabbits and squirrels."

"That's his nature." Star shrugged. "We cannot expect

him to live on squash and dried persimmons."

"A dog!" squealed Richie. "Oh, Hildy! We're going to have a dog!" Clearly, with Beth's advent and now a dog, his four-and-a-half-year-old life had brightened tremendously.

With an ache in her throat, Christy hugged Beth. How would these children and countless like them grow up after what they'd seen, after the death of parents, the savage destruction of their worlds?

Once again she blessed the valley. If only Dan O'Brien, her sweetheart, and Charlie were here! But they were men and had to fight their battles. *I'll fight mine, too,* Christy resolved, straightening from her sister. *I'll stay at the happy house. If anyone, jayhawk or bushwhacker, burns it, I'll rig a shelter under the big tree, the way we lived when we first came. And as long as I have food or a roof, I'll share them as Father and Mother did, the way Star shares with us.*

Christy untangled her sister's wild curls. "Take care of Richie and help Mother while I'm gone, Beth."

Beth thrust out her lower lip and shot an annoyed look at her oblivious sister-in-law. "I'm Joely's aunt! I want to take care of him, but M'lissa won't let me."

Small wonder that Melissa clung to her baby. Within a week, she'd lost mother, father, home, everything familiar excepting Phronie and Lilah. Christy dropped on one knee to gaze into Beth's hazel eyes. "You can help a lot with Joely when he's a little bigger. Right now you can help best by not pestering Melissa and doing good things like gathering wood and kindling for the fires."

Ellen nodded. "You'll have chores here, just as you did at home. And we'll have lessons."

"Lessons?" Beth's lips quivered. "But . . . Father was the teacher. . . ."

"I am now," said Ellen. She included the other women

with an encompassing gesture and smiled. "All of us are."

Promising not to forget Robbie, Sarah and Christy made the steep ascent to the river cave. "Powerful lot of teachers for two children," Sarah mused as they passed from the light and lit their candles. "But when you think about it, look at all they know . . . Phronie and Lilah and Hildy have been slaves. Your mother can teach reading and ciphering and such. Star knows how to live in the valley and the old Osage ways I hope she'll teach me."

"Are you going to live in the valley?"

"Aren't you?"

"No. I'll go back and forth, of course, but I'm staying outside," Christy answered.

Sarah didn't speak for a time. Then she asked: "Why?"

"Because . . ."—it was hard to put into words—"I guess I can't stand to turn things over to the Watt Caxtons, Doc Jennisons, Jim Lanes, and especially not to the likes of Lafe Ballard." Lafe who loved pain, who, at the raising of the happy house, had deliberately pushed her wrist against a searing hot kettle. She still wore that brand. Worse, he had carved his initials on Dan's dear face after killing Andy McHugh on the bloody hill above Wilson's Creek. Apparently Lafe had served his brief stint in the Confederate Army and then had gone into the less dangerous and more lucrative career of riding with guerrillas. He'd been with the band that had killed Christy's father.

Sarah nodded slowly. "How can a wonderful lady like Hester have such a varmint for a son? You say she doesn't know he was with the gang when they killed Emil Franz and Lottie?

"When she brought the wounded man to us, she said one man in the group that hung Emil looked like Lafe, but wasn't."

"Well, let's hope she never has to remember." Sarah's smooth jaw hardened. "You'll try to farm?"

"I'll try."

"If you manage to raise a crop, one thieving bunch or another will steal the grain or turn their horses loose on it."

"If it's early enough, I'll plant again. If it's too late, then spring will come."

"And so will they! Union, Secesh, or just plain robbers!"

Christy again saw Caxton blasting her father down, watched that awful crumpling, arms still extended in welcome. If she'd had a shotgun. . . . Yes, glad and gladly she'd have killed Watt Caxton if she could have. The rage in her heart when she thought of him did not belong in Peace Valley.

"Whoever comes, I'll stay."

"Then I'll stay, too, though I want to visit Star and hear all she can tell me about our people." Sarah laughed. "I like belonging to the Sky People, and I don't think Blessed Mary or her Son mind a bit. I'll fetch my bees to your place. Star doesn't need them."

"You don't have to stay with me."

"I've had enough of my own company, what with Lige gone." Sarah hesitated. "I remember your cabin-raising and how we made the quilt while the sill boards were laid on the foundation. While we stitched and talked, the walls went up."

"They only used nails on the roof," Christy remembered. "Andy McHugh made them." She swallowed hard, thinking of Andy's red-haired baby boy who'd never know his father, killed at Wilson's Creek. *Please, please! Let Joely know Charlie!*

"I wonder if that'll ever happen again," Sarah mused. "Neighbor men raising a cabin or barn or trading work at harvest while the women make a quilt and put together a feast?"

Christy thought of her father, how he expected good from people and usually met with it. Till that last day. *Will it always hurt this much? How does Mother stand it?* "We have to believe that someday neighbors will help each other again," Christy said. "Anyway, Star has welcomed us, and you and Hester are helping us. . . ."

"Ourselves, too," Sarah insisted. "One good thing, the hounds will set up such a racket that no one's going to sneak up on us."

The women were growing familiar enough with the sinuous cavern to traverse it more speedily, especially unhampered by burdens. As the azure sky shone from the entrance, they blew out their candles and walked slowly to accustom their eyes to the brightness. Perhaps, too, Sarah, like Christy, needed time to change from the timeless underground, with neither day, night, season, or weather, to the outer world, so different from the valley.

Hester Ballard, across the creek, stood in the winter orchard, her hands on the branches, as if she would warm the buds into life. A cloud of cedar waxwings dropped into their namesake trees edging the cornfield beyond Jonathan Ware's grave, and a brilliant red male cardinal flew from a tree to offer a berry to his demurely hued mate on the fence. A busy, happy, beautiful world, in spite of what had happened here, in spite of the oblong of broken sod at the edge of the stubble.

Christy and Sarah told an amazed and delighted Hester about the valley, Star, and Hildy while they fitted the raucous Wyandottes into covered willow baskets, haltered Lad and the dry cows, and fastened corn-shuck mattresses on the animals' backs, holding them down by roped baskets of indignant chickens.

Christy hated not to keep Dan's fiddle near her. At least she could polish it and remember his long skillful fingers holding it and drawing the bow. It was too risky, though, to have it where raiders might break or steal it, so she nestled the fiddle in its battered case into one of the mattresses and secured it firmly.

"I'd admire to see that valley and meet Star," said Hester, adding a bag of turnips to Lad's burden. "And that little fair-haired boy. . . ."

"Why don't you go with Sarah?" Christy asked.

"But that man in there. . . ."

"Isn't he still sleeping most of the time? He doesn't even need to know you're gone. Stay as long as you like."

"I'm mending his shirt."

"I'll finish it. Won't even leave a needle, sticking out, to jab him."

When Hester still hesitated, Sarah touched Christy's arm. "I'll come back tonight. Dark makes no never mind in the cave, and I don't mind it, anyway."

So while the younger women started the animals toward the entrance, Hester got her things together. Robbie wanted to turn back when Christy did, but she gave him a hug and pointed at the procession. "Run along, pup. Beth wants you . . . and so does a little boy!"

He went, glancing back with inquiring whines. Christy watched them vanish except for the candles' flickering. She'd look in on the wounded man before she milked Guinevere, who, not much comforted by the presence of Lass and the wounded man's black horse, lowed unhappily after her companions.

Going to the bedroom cabin, Christy froze at the sight of the empty bed. A soft laugh came from the bench by the window. "You sure have been busy, Christy Ware. Is there a big room in that cave where you're hiding all the critters?"

The stranger they had nursed through violent fever was cleaning his revolver with the care and tenderness of a lover. With an effort, Christy kept from shuddering. Even before her father's life was blasted away by a gun, Christy had a fear of guns.

"You've been spying!"

He quirked a dark eyebrow. "Wouldn't say that, Miss Christy. I just wasn't asleep all the time Miz Ballard thought I was."

She thought of the valley, of her family taking refuge there with Star and Hildy. This man wasn't going to carry his war to that hidden place. If she had to, she'd find a way to kill him.

"There's a cow and mare left here," she said. "Can't you be satisfied with them?"

"Why, Miss Christy, do you think I'd steal from you ladies after you saved my life?"

Almost going limp, she said faintly: "I hope you wouldn't."

"Depend on it." Reading her thoughts, he gave a disarming grin. "I won't tell the boys."

"Thank you."

"Least I can do."

Putting the gun aside, he got to his feet and crossed the space between them. Hester had shaved him or he had done it himself. His salty male odor was not unpleasant, thanks to her mother's soap, and it stirred an awareness in Christy as unwelcome as it was sudden and unexpected. He wore a shirt of her father's, buttoned only part way to accommodate the dressings of his wound. The muscles in his tanned throat and shoulders flexed as he dropped his hands on her shoulders and the blue blaze of his eyes engulfed her.

"You were wondering how to kill me. Weren't you, Christy Ware?"

His amusement stung. Warmth pulsed from his fingers through her body. *Dan! Dan!* It took all her strength to step back. The man didn't try to hold her. He just watched her with those brilliant dark-centered eyes.

"I . . . I'd have to kill you if I didn't believe you'll keep your word."

"I'll keep it. Who knows? I might need to hide in your cave someday."

This man in the valley?

He laughed at her dismay, lifted her chin with a caressing hand. "Have you got a sweetheart, Miss Christy?"

How to answer?

Her face had. He released her. "I reckon he's fighting for the Union?"

"Yes."

His smile was crooked. "Guess the best thing I can wish for you is that he gets hurt enough to get sent home, but not hurt so bad you'll be sorry he was." The dark young man sat down on the bed. "Dog-gone it! Still weak as a kitten."

"You're lucky you're alive!" Christy couldn't keep from saying it. "My father isn't. A gang of guerrillas rode in here, killed my father, killed the sheep and hogs, and stole close to everything."

The blackness in the center of his eyes covered the blue. "Your pa must have been a Union man."

"He was, but that was no excuse to kill him when he stood in his own door and welcomed the riders."

His eyes veiled. "Christy Ware, I'm sorry about your pa," he said at last. "Will you be sorry for my pa, too? A squad of Union soldiers hanged him, along with my uncle for sympathizing with the South."

Christy gave an involuntary cry. She could no longer hold back her tears. "Where does it end? You're here because your father was killed. My brothers are fighting, one on either side. My sister-in-law's family was burned out by Union soldiers. I expect we'll be burned out by men like you. . . ."

"Maybe for you it ends here . . . with you taking care of me in spite of everything." He touched her hand briefly, and let out a sighing breath. "I'll send the word around that anyone who bothers you or this farm answers to me, Bill Anderson. Not many would care to do that, not even Quantrill."

The name meant nothing to her, although he seemed to think it would. "I suppose I have to thank you."

His teeth flashed. "Don't choke on it. I promise you that I'll kill every jayhawk and bluebelly I can."

"My brother. . . ."

"If I knew he was your brother, I wouldn't kill him if I could help it, Miss Ware. But men don't swap calling cards in the middle of a fight. You could tear off the bandage now and let me bleed to death. I'm weaker'n a cat and I don't even have claws." His eyelids drooped, lashes thick on his cheeks.

"Don't be silly. Rest, and, when you wake up, you'll get some pudding."

He grinned faintly. "You sound like Josie, too. My sister loves to spoil me."

Christy looked down at the man, wondering with a pang where her own were, praying they were alive and well and had warm clothing. And Dan. Where was he? And David Parks and Theo Wattles? She was relieved when Sarah returned while she was ladling up the stew, and more relieved when Sarah and Bill took a liking to each other and bantered as if they'd grown up together.

Lighting a candle so she could see to mend his shirt, Christy realized she was almost enjoying his company. They were like survivors of wrecked enemy ships washed up on an island, united by the will to live and their youth. Bill, he admitted, was only twenty, the same age as Thos, her brother, a year younger than Dan. If they lived through the war, would these young men be able to pick up the lives they should have led or would they miss battle and danger?

"Your sister made you a beautiful shirt," she told Bill as she repaired the stem of an embroidered rose.

"Josie's a rare hand with a needle. Maybe someday I'll bring her to see you."

"I hope you can," Christy said.

CHAPTER THREE

Christmas came. Bill Anderson had ridden off on his black horse, turning in the saddle to wave a good bye. Lilah had had a baby girl—very fair-skinned—she had named Noelle. All the animals and chickens were now in the valley for safety and so Christy and Sarah could go there for a visit. At noon, everyone, except Lilah, was gathered under the broad overhang of the unwalled front of the newcomers' cave. Delicious odors wafted from three Dutch ovens nestled in the coals of a fire built in a rock oblong that accommodated a large coffee pot at one end.

It was good to sing again, although it hurt to think of how Jonathan Ware would have loved to learn the Osage hymns. Christy could almost see him, throat swelling lustily, auburn head thrown back. How could someone so alive, so joyous in this world, suddenly not exist? His body was returning to the soil at the edge of his cornfield, but where had his spirit gone?

Jonathan's faith had had to do with how to live on this earth with its fellow creatures. He had never talked much about the afterlife beyond maintaining that God was too good to send anyone to hell. Her straying thoughts were caught in his favorite carol as her mother's clear voice led it.

Mary and Joseph walked in an orchard good
Where was cherries and berries as red as any blood. . . .

Then Joseph's fury at being cuckolded: "If he's a man

can get a child, he's a man can climb a tree. Go tell you that man, and tell him speedily, that cherries and berries mean nothing to me." The babe, from his mother's womb, commanding the cherry tree to bow down to her hand. Joseph's awed contrition when he realized his innocent wife was with child by God.

"Every child is born with God in him," Christy's father used to say. "It's men who call some bastards."

Why, you are with us, Father! Christy thought. *As long as we remember how you lived and what you said, you live in us. You'll be in your grandchildren, too, though you'll never know them, because Charlie and Thos and Beth and I will tell them about you. What's more important, we'll live the way you taught us.* Christy wanted to call this out to her mother, but, when she caught her mother's eye, she was sure she already knew it.

Richie settled into Hester's arms. She held him loosely as if he were sunlight, brown head bent to his golden one. Surely she was remembering Lafe at that sweet age before something took over and turned him mean.

From beneath a blanket, Star produced two stick horses. Their heads were cut from chunks of sycamore limb that still had white bark on them, flaps of it peeled up to shape pricked ears. Shredded bark fibers wedged tight in grooves made creditable manes, and the eyes were black pebbles glued into hollows filled with pine resin.

"Now you can ride your ponies all over the valley," she said. "But, mind you, lean them against the wall when you're not galloping so that no one trips over them."

While Beth and Richie charged off toward the river, whooping and hollering, Star raised the blanket from what could only be Joely's cradleboard. She smiled as she brought it to Melissa, brass hawk bells fastened to the

56

hooded top of the board, jingling gaily. "Cedar stands for eternal life. A cradle of it should bless your son with many years. I made the hood with part of my last buffalo robe."

Melissa gazed at the present with a stunned expression. To cover the silence, Christy touched what was probably a cardinal's scarlet feather attached to the head of the board next to the striped wing feather of a woodpecker, and a blue one that could have come from a grosbeak, jay, or bluebird. She couldn't identify the bits of fluff tied to the hawk bells.

"What beautiful feathers!"

"It makes a small star's eyes keen to have something to watch," the guardian said. She didn't seem to notice Melissa's strange behavior.

Ellen took the baby from Phronie's arms and handed him to Star. "Will you show us how to lace him in? I wish I'd had one of these when my children were little!"

Star regarded Joely's flannel gown and diaper with disfavor and tilted the board to show the soft dry moss in the bottom half. "Moss soaks up the child's messes and keeps him comfortable till his mother cleans him and puts in clean moss. With that thing"—she touched the diaper—"he will cry, and his skin will get sore if he's not changed right away."

"He will be!" Melissa almost snapped.

Star said no more but left the moss in place, doubtless hoping it would keep the cedar's fragrance from being overpowered. Taking Joely, she crooned to him softly as she placed him on the board.

Melissa, watching with dilated eyes, suddenly cried: "No!" She snatched up the baby. Startled, he began to yowl as she ran away with him, not to Star's cave, but to the one where Lilah drowsed. With a shake of her grizzled head, Phronie went after her.

"I'm so sorry!" Ellen's face was crimson. "I beg your pardon for my daughter-in-law, Star. Losing her home and parents has made her . . . not herself."

"She is very much herself." There was no censure in Star's tone. "She fears her son will become a savage. That is too bad. He would feel safe and happy laced snug on the board, carried on our backs or hung by the loop to a tree limb. But Lilah will be glad of the gift, I think."

Beth and Richie were trotting back, Beth slowing to let the younger child reach the grown-ups first. "Oh, Star!" she begged, hazel eyes glowing. "Give our ponies some Osage names!"

Star considered. "How about Gleh-mon? That means Arrow Flying Home. And Wind, perhaps? I-ba-tse Ta'dse."

Richie stroked his mount's fibrous mane. "Gleh-mon! He my Arrow. Can't say the Wind name."

"I can!" Beth scratched between her steed's bark ears. "It's like a rhyme! I-ba-tse Ta'dse!" Her eyes widened as Sarah presented her with the elegantly doll-sized, fringed, and beaded buckskin dress and moccasins. "For Lynette? Oh, Sarah, thank you! She'll love being an Osage princess!" Beth caught Star's hand. "Could we put spiders on her hands, just like yours?"

Star looked quizzical. "Spiders would look strange when your doll wears white lady clothes."

Melissa wouldn't like it one bit, having her favorite doll marked with what she'd think a heathen symbol. "Maybe," Christy suggested, "we can paint spiders on with pokeberry juice . . . something that'll wash off."

Richie, enthralled with Lige's whistle, hooted eerie owl cries till Beth lured him away to play with Thos's marbles and experiment with catching the ball in the small wooden cup and spinning the hickory top. Christy stitched on

Lambie's soft new covering with long-lashed embroidered eyes, and the gifting was complete.

Phronie marched her nursling along the path. "I beg your pardon, Star." Melissa was shamefaced but defiant. "It's very kind of you to make Joely such a beautiful gift. But I. . . ."

Star gently cut her off. "The cradleboard is the beginning of the Road of Life. It is your right to decide which road to set him on."

Gathered by the Dutch ovens with their plates, they all bowed their heads while Ellen, in a voice that wavered a few times but then resonated, thanked God for their food, for health, and for this valley.

Then Star raised her arms to the sky and thanked Wah' Kon-Tah for brightening their lives with two little stars on this day of the birth of his own beloved Son. The rest of them raised their arms, too. Christy had to admit that offering herself to the heavens with embracing arms, filling her lungs with the air that nourished all life, made her feel closer to God, Great Mystery, or whatever one called the power, than did closing her eyes and lowering her head.

"Here in winter, we know spring will come," Star finished. "Thank you, Grandfather, for the winter that lets us joy in spring."

Facing the sky, Christy made a silent prayer. *I'm glad we had Father as long as we did. I'm grateful for his life. Thank you for him. Thank you for his grandson. Help me protect the place he loved, plow and plant his fields so he'll hear the rustling corn. Help us make it a happy house again that welcomes everyone.*

By evening, the sky clouded. There was a scurry to bring wood into the caves or store it under overhangs. Christy and Sarah milked the cows that sheltered with the other cattle and horses under a grotto-like overhang where Hildy, Beth, and Richie had cut and piled up quantities of dried grass. Hildy and the children shut the chickens in their roost cave with heaped-up boughs and brush.

"I'm glad we brought Guinevere and Lass," said Christy. "I'm sure they're happier with their friends, and we don't have to worry about getting back to milk."

Snow fell faster, soft and noiseless as an owl's fringed wing. Near the blazing, cedar-pungent fire in the new cave, the remains of the noon feast tasted delicious. Noelle slept soundly, laced into the cradleboard leaning against a rock. Lilah sat up with pillows between her and the wall. Melissa was silent, but at least she was there.

Before she got in bed with Beth that night, Christy got Dan's fiddle out of the safe niche she'd found for it, took it out of its case along with his precious letter, and held them against her. The letter smelled of wood smoke and tobacco although Dan didn't use it.

Dan, oh, Danny, be well . . . come back to us. Come back.

The strings made a sound like a lonesome wind.

The Christmas storm was the beginning of weeks of rain, sleet, and more snow. To lessen the number in the cave, Christy and Sarah went back to the Ware home at the first break in the weather. It was well they did. Owen Parks rode up on Breeze that afternoon, hailing the house. When Christy answered, he put the bay gelding in the barn out of the drizzle, and ran to the house, panting good naturedly as he pelted across the threshold.

"My womenfolk have been hoping for decent weather so they could visit, but it seemed a shame not to get these letters to you, and this package." With a flourish, he pulled two crumpled letters and a small packet from inside his coat. "Two from Dan and one from Thos. We didn't get a scratch from that rascal, Davie. Maybe Dan will say what he's up to."

"Read your letters," Sarah bade Christy. "Take off your coat, Mister Parks, and warm yourself while I brew some wild rose hip tea." She smiled at the dismay in the handsome young man's brown eyes. "It's quite nice with a little honey and helps ward off colds," she added, and hung his coat on a chair a prudent distance from the fire and swung the cast-iron water kettle over the flames. Two kettles salvaged from Rose Haven were in the valley, so this one could remain at the cabin.

Skipping the parts of Dan's letters that made her blush happily, Christy shared the rest. Captain John Brown, Jr., had arrived from Ohio with the rest of Company K and taken up his command, although greatly plagued by rheumatism. Doc Jennison had no desire to stay in winter camp near West Point with his men, but had turned up with his wife a few days after Christmas to be entertained by stirring music from the twenty-two regimental buglers.

Colonel Dan Anthony, who was in command, had heard several hundred guerrillas were in Dayton, Missouri. They were gone when he got there New Year's Day of 1862 with 200 men and a howitzer, but, since the town had allowed guerrillas to gather there, Anthony burned forty-five of Dayton's forty-six houses. The spared one belonged to a Union man who had somehow managed to stick it out amongst his Secessionist neighbors.

I have no stomach for such doings, Dan wrote. *Rather drive mules and pry wagons out of the mud. Please tell Uncle Simeon and the family that Davie isn't writing because a mule's heel connected with his hand the other day. Didn't break anything, but he can't hold a pencil. He's the best teamster we've got, except for Thos, which is a great marvel to the rest of the boys since neither of them whip their beasts or turn the air purple.*

"So Davie's all right." Owen sighed with relief. "I could almost feel sorry for him, skinning mules instead of flourishing a saber, but I hate to think how Pa would worry if the boy was in an outfit facing battle." Sipping the lemon-scented tea and munching on a persimmon sugarplum, he glanced around the room that was much barer without Ellen Ware's piano and the carved family rocker. "Father and the women want you and Missus Ware to know that you're welcome at the mill." He shook his head wonderingly. "It's hard to believe your mother's really living in a cave, Christy. And Melissa Jardine . . . I mean Melissa Ware!"

"Melissa's the only one who seems to hate it, but she'd not be happy anywhere right now. I wish we could get her to her sister in Saint Louis."

Owen considered. "She could take the stage to Leavenworth and get on a steamer there that would take her down the Missouri to the city."

"Yes, but that would be a great deal out of the way . . . a very hard trip with the baby . . . and expensive."

"Most of our customers pay in kind, not cash," Owen said, "but some do buy flour, and so do the Trading Post store and the Army camp close to there. I reckon we have money enough for your sister-in-law's journey."

"You're kind, Owen," Christy responded, "and thank you. But if Melissa still wants to leave, when the weather's fit for travel, we'll take her to Sedalia and the train."

Owen frowned. "Let me drive. It's too dangerous for women to jaunter about alone."

"I think it's much more dangerous for men. So far neither side's killing women on purpose."

When Owen rode away, clearly unhappy about leaving two women by themselves, even though Christy had told him about Bill Anderson's promise of protection, she read again the more personal parts of Dan's letter. *Thank you for the splendid handkerchiefs, mittens, and socks. My others were worn to pieces. These will keep me warm, doubly warm because you made them, but, oh, how much I'd rather be warmed by holding you, my darling. You're always in my mind and heart but most especially when I roll up in your blanket. Please do think of me then. We haven't been paid and there's not much I'd like to give you in the Fort Scott stores, anyway, but I did whittle this locket for you out of cedar. I'm afraid it smells nicer than it looks, but I can't tell you how many pieces I ruined trying to make something that looked more like a rose than a cauliflower. The cord's braided out of hairs from Raven's tail. He's a beautiful black artillery horse I hope I get to ride if I ever get out of driving mules.*

Christy pressed the wood to her cheek, smiling as she pictured Dan squinting at the design in fierce concentration. Placed around her neck, the horsehair cord chafed a little, but nothing, nothing, had ever been more precious.

CHAPTER FOUR

Beth said the valley was magic because of Star, and Star was magic because of the valley. Beth said Richie could be her little brother, and that Robbie was his dog, too, although Robbie might not know that since he still slept beside Beth. It was nice to have a sister although Richie couldn't see why she thought the babies were fun and why she liked to hold them, not when she could be pulling him on the sled Aunt Sarah had made, or playing marbles or make-believe. Still, she was a much more satisfactory sister than Alice who was old, at least as old as Hildy, and his really big, big brother, Edmund.

Richie cried sometimes because his mama couldn't hug him and tuck him in at night, and he got a peculiar hurting inside when he remembered how his papa would pretend to be a bear and wrestle with him or hold him in his lap and read him stories. He missed Aunt Becky and all his playmates, but he loved having his own cozy little sleeping hollow in the wall above the main cave.

Mr. Bun lived in a nook and there were plenty of ledges for treasures, the little box with his mother's hair, his eight favorite soldiers, and now the owl whistle, marbles, and top. Living in the valley was like playing make-believe all the time, especially since Star was a real Indian. Aunt Sarah's mother had been Indian, but she acted pretty much like Aunt Christy and Aunt Ellen.

There certainly were a lot of aunts! Aunt Phronie was the main one since all the others called her that, except for

Aunt Lilah who called her Grandma. Star had told him and Beth that she liked to be called just that. Hildy stayed Hildy to him, but was Aunt Hildy to Beth. The good thing, in Richie's view, was that all the women treated him like their own little boy, except for Aunt Melissa who hardly ever smiled except at Joely or her dumb, old cat, Emmy, who hissed at Richie and scratched him hard the time he tried to pick her up.

Aunt Hester hugged him and told him Emmy was a nasty grouch who didn't deserve to be petted. She put good-smelling salve on the scratches that stopped the hurting. When his legs were worn out from trotting after Beth, Aunt Hester held him and sang about how froggie went a-courting, weevily wheat, skipping to my Lou, and the jolly miller boy. He was too big to nap, but sometimes he went to sleep in Aunt Hester's arms and it was like being in his mama's arms again. Aunt Hester told him her boy was grown up, so she was especially glad to have him to love—and he knew her love was somehow different from the kindness the other aunties had for him.

He could read lots of words in Aunt Ellen's primer, print his name and Beth's and Robbie's, count to twenty, and add or take away from the pebbles he and Beth used to do sums. They had school for what seemed a long time, every morning. Every afternoon, Beth was supposed to write in her journal, so usually he did, too, at least he drew pictures, and Beth and one of the aunts would help him spell the words he needed. Most of his journal was about what Star showed them.

She read the outdoors like Aunt Ellen read the hardest, longest words. She knew whether rabbits or deer had gnawed twigs because rabbits make sharp cuts but deer leave raggedy edges. If tracks in the snow were too blurred to tell what made them—a raccoon or 'possum—Star knew a raccoon never drags its tail although a 'possum often does.

She knew stories about all the creatures, and a dandy one about the great big woodpecker, the one with the bright red topknot. "When the Sky People first traveled west on the plains, they were driven back by fierce, pale-skinned warriors who wore buffalo horn headdresses," Star said. "The Sky People had to run away, and that made them feel bad. While they rested at their fire that evening, the great woodpecker flew up and called to them. They saw he was black as night except for white marks of day and his splendid crest that was the color of Father Fire.

"He had come to be their guardian on the plains. They shot him with a blunted bird arrow and put his skin in a rush bag the leader could carry around his neck. The head they skinned, also, and hung it from the sacred pipe. After that, they were not afraid on the plains, though they sometimes had to fight the pale warriors."

Star took Beth and Richie to watch an otter family play on their slide on a slope above the river at the far end of the valley. Five of the sleek, small-eared creatures, who were longer than Richie, took turns tucking their forepaws close to their bodies, launching themselves, on their bellies, down the icy bank, shooting into the water, then bobbing up and again making their way to the top. They had a snow wallow, too, where you could see the print of their webbed, clawed feet.

"I wish I could slide with them," Richie said once to Beth.

"Silly Billy! You wouldn't like winding up in that cold river! Come on, let's go see what's happening at the hotel."

The hotel was almost as much fun as the otters. It was a

giant dead tree, charred down the side by lightning that had set it afire. Rain must have doused the flames quickly along the scarred slash because loosened bark was gradually peeling off the rest of the trunk and, in places, was held only by the gnarled grip of a huge grapevine that twined and looped to the stubbed upper branches. There was perched what Beth called an "e-nor-mous" mass of dry leaves and twigs. It probably belonged to the dark gray squirrels that popped in and out of several hollows, chattering irately at their visitors. They had the most beautiful fluffy white-fringed tails that stretched out behind them when they sailed through the air, curled around them when they dozed, slowed their downward plummet if they fell, and arched handsomely over them when they paused to relish a nut.

Woodpeckers drummed as they pillaged the bark crevices for larvae, the Osages' magic crested one who seemed to live in the tree; the jaunty little white-fronted, black-masked sort with white bars almost like rounded checks on his black wings and a small red band at the back of his head, and his larger but similar-looking relative. Black-capped nuthatches moved jerkily down the bark, headfirst.

A 'possum occupied one cavity halfway up the trunk. Once, the children glimpsed her sitting on her hind legs and funny bare tail on a nearby limb, licking herself like Emmy did. Star said her babies would be born soon and live in her pouch, hanging onto the nipples on which life depended, till they were big enough to venture out. There often weren't enough nipples for all the babies. Star said the weak ones would never live to grow up, but Richie couldn't see why there should be any weak ones.

There was a mysterious hole burrowed under one snarl of roots with a heap of earth beside it. Richie and Beth hoped it was a fox, but Star thought it was likely *otchek,* the woodchuck, snoozing away the winter in his grassy bed after feeding so fat on greens he could scarcely waddle.

All around were marvels. Flocks of rusty-breasted bluebirds shimmered like patches of the bluest sky as they settled to feed on dried berries in thickets beyond the tree. There were flocks of robins, too, and goldfinches caught any sun there was as they perched to dine on thistles.

Perhaps the most interesting thing of all was the bear log. The day Star took them to see it, she told them to tie Robbie so he couldn't follow. "It's not wise to wake up this mother," she warned as they neared the great log that thrust broken, rotted roots far higher than her head. "Be quiet now. Quiet as falling snow, and step as lightly."

When they stood beside the scarred, peeling trunk, she pressed her ear against it and motioned for them to do the same. From within the wood came a happy, buzzing sound.

"Bees?" Richie started to ask, but Star touched his lips to close them and moved silently away. When they were quite a distance from the log, she said: "That sound was the baby bears nursing. There are probably two of them. Farther north I've heard bears sleep sound all winter, but here they wander around between long naps. The cubs are born tiny and almost naked. Their mother won't bring them out till it's warmer."

"Oh, can we see them then?" cried Beth.

"Probably, but from a safe distance. Don't come here without me. Mother bears take great care of their babies. She might think you mean them harm."

Above these secrets of woods and river was the sky. Bald eagles, white-headed and white-tailed, that roosted at night in trees along the river, soared with flat wings till they were gleaming pinpoints or played and tumbled in currents of air, much as the otters reveled on their slide. Ospreys vied with them for fish, but the red-tailed hawks, that had a big stick nest in an oak not far from the bear log, circled for mice or rabbits, or even smaller birds.

Just as the air kingdom was different from those of water or earth, night brought a different world. When Moon Woman glowed or when her face was hidden, the song of wolves came faintly from above the valley, a panther might scream like a woman, a bobcat or fox crush the dying shriek of a smaller creature. When such sounds came, Richie hugged Mr. Bun tighter and was glad Star, Aunt Hester, Hildy, and the rest of the aunties were near.

As flesh-hunters stalked forest and meadow, the clans of the Owl People ruled the air: the tiny screech owl trilling as darkness fell; the barn owl with its heart-shaped face gliding over the meadow; the great horned owl uttering its hunger cry that sounded much like Emmy's shriek if her tail were trod on. Star said this owl's wings spread as wide as she was tall, and it could sweep up a fox or big turkey in its steel talons. This made Richie afraid to use his owl whistle after twilight. He didn't want the owl to get him.

Living so near wild things was exciting, but Richie was glad of the cattle and horses, even the chickens, because they reminded him of a home that grew hazier each time he tried to remember it but that still mattered deep inside, just as he'd always be his mama's own boy no matter how much he loved his aunts, Star, and Hildy. He helped Beth pull grass for the animals to store for when snow covered the ground, and helped gather the eggs and shut the chickens up before twilight. Three had been killed and eaten, but, when they saw the shadow of a hawk, they squawked an alarm and made for their shelter.

Early in what Aunt Hester's almanac called February,

Richie and Beth watched a flutter of small violet-blue butterflies hover around swelling buds on purplish dogwood
twigs. The butterflies were a chance delight on a visit to a
small pond where a turtle foraged amid fresh green spikes of
cat-tail. The pond flickered with tadpoles and from all
around rose a sound like the jingling of the hawk bells on
Noelle's cradleboard. How spring peepers, brown frogs no
longer than his little finger, could make such a racket was
beyond Richie.

"Hear the chickadees?" Star was carrying several bark
troughs and baskets. "They're building nests and singing
for their mates now, not just having conversations. They're
also telling other birds not to come near their nests. Cardi-
nals will be the next to set up housekeeping, and then wives
will join the red-winged blackbirds who'll be here soon."

Richie tip-toed to peer in the troughs. Star smiled at his
disgusted sigh and ruffled his hair. "They won't be empty
long, Sun Boy."

That was her name for him. Richie liked it. It made him
feel Indian. Of course, he *was* Indian, three-sixteenths.
Hildy tried to show him by counting out sixteen twigs.
"Your daddy be four of these." She set four to one side.
"Your mama be two. You get two parts from him, one from
her . . . three parts, see? That's how much Cherokee you
are. The rest from your daddy is a kind of white . . . from
Scotland long ago . . . and from your mama, there's English
and French."

Richie stared at his smooth pale honey-colored hand. "I
don't look that mixed up, Hildy."

"Lord, child, you're nothin' compared to some white
folks who've got a sprinkle of well nigh everything." She
drew herself up proudly. "My daddy, he was pure
Coromantee, my mama, Mandingo with likely some Arab."

It was a puzzlement to Richie that Aunt Phronie, Aunt Lilah, and Hildy were all "colored"—they said so themselves—when Lilah's skin was fairer than that of any of his aunts, save Melissa. That was one of the grown-up riddles he supposed he wouldn't understand till he was grown-up, too.

Touching the side of a bark trough, he looked up at Star. "What are you goin' to put in them, Star?"

"Come and see." She left the baskets near the pond and started for the timber. "As we walk, see how the buds on most of the bushes and trees have started to swell."

"Why?" asked Richie.

"It's warm enough that sap's starting to rise through the trunks and branches to the twigs. That makes the leaves open, though the redbud will get its flowers before it has leaves. Now is the time to ask the maples to share their sweet juice. It's one of the best gifts of Wah'-kon-ta."

"Maple syrup!" Beth squealed. "Hayeses used to trade us some for eggs and butter!"

"Oh, look at the deer!" Richie pointed. "They're eating the twigs!"

How beautiful the deer were with their big ears and white tails! Three of them stretched graceful necks to browse the parts of trees they could reach. At Robbie's approach, they bounded away, one with swollen sides behind the others.

"She'll have her fawns soon," Star said. Taking her knife from its sheath, she made two cuts that came together at a sharp downward point. Shaving a stick to a point, she drove this into the bottom of the slashes. "Now put the trough where the sap will drip down in it from the stick," she said.

They did the same to another tree, and then Star took them to the pond and put them to gathering watercress in one basket while she waded into the cat-tails and slipped her hand down along one stalk into the water. "You don't want to pull on just the stalk," she explained. "It'll break off and leave some of the best parts in the mud."

She yanked out a big brownish root and placed it with the stalk at the edge of the pond, pulled up three more rope-like roots, rinsed them, and trimmed off small white shoots that she dropped in her basket. "This lump the stalk grows out of is very good." She cut what looked something like a potato free of stalk and root and added it to her harvest. Next, she cut off the green top of the stalk and tossed it away along with so many layers of the stalk that it seemed nothing would be left. "This part . . . only the inner three or four rings . . . is tender. Beth, Sun Boy, I'll trim the rest of the stalks and you may peel them."

Richie wasn't sure about eating cat-tails that evening, but he was sure he didn't want to aggravate Star. He pretended he was all Indian, not just three-sixteenths, and tasted of the inner stalks, root shoots, and lumps sliced and cooked in butter and a cream soup of watercress and sheep sorrel.

"It's good!" He blinked in surprise. "Let's have this every day! There's lots of cat-tails!"

"Yes, and we want to leave plenty to grow," said Star. "When the spikes are green, we'll boil some and eat them like roasting ears. When the spikes turn brown and are gold with pollen, we'll shake it off and use it like flour. Cat-tails have something good from spring till autumn."

It snowed that night. Star, with Robbie, kept watch by the sap troughs for many wild creatures would revel in the sweetness. When Richie and Beth plunged knee-deep through snow turned to frosted rose by the dawn, Star was lifting a chunk of ice from one trough.

"The water from the sap freezes. What's left is thicker, sweeter, and stronger flavored. It still needs to be boiled to make syrup or sugar, but freezing saves a lot of time. Here, I'll make you some candy."

She dipped blobs of the sap on the snow. It hardened to wonderful chewiness. Not even Richie's mother's French chocolates had tasted so good!

"Now," Star said as the children licked their fingers, "gather the driest wood you can find and bring it here while I fetch a kettle. We'll start boiling this batch while the troughs fill again."

That night, they had a special treat—pancakes of their hoarded wheat flour, rich with pecans and chunks of dried persimmon, drizzled with hot syrup. It was still thin, but made the pancakes so delicious that Richie ate till he couldn't hold another bite.

Curled up in Aunt Hester's arms, lulled by the sound of her heart and breathing as much as by her songs, he cuddled Mr. Bun, sighed blissfully, and drifted off to sleep.

CHAPTER FIVE

It was a good thing that over the past five years Jonathan Ware and the boys had plowed up most of the rocks and cleared away the stumps. Now that the ground had thawed, Christy could hold the plowshare deep enough to cut a respectable furrow as she followed Lad and Lass under the cold moon. Sarah had stayed in the valley to help with the last of the maple sap boiling and the cutting of bark for the lodge they'd build before winter, but the hounds sprawled at the edge of the field, and they were company as well as sentries.

At first the bleached light and weird shadows made Christy nervous, but, as the horses' hoofs clomped on earth that opened to the share with pungent richness and as she watched the team move willingly along in spite of the strange hour, she fell into the age-old rhythm, the reassuring familiarity of carrying out the proper work of the season.

Plowing, planting, cultivating, harvest, storing for the winter. Late freezes, heavy rains, drought, blight, and grasshoppers, or other plagues might damage or ruin a crop, but these themselves came at certain times and were part of nature whose scourges must be accepted as well as her bounty.

War had no season. It destroyed all the others, savaged the pattern of planting and reaping, killed young men rather than old. And these young men, instead of planting and tending it, trampled the young corn, looted the harvest, ravaged in minutes what they knew had taken months of work to grow. It was because of this chaos that Christy had to plow by night and hide the horses in the timber by day.

Still, she was plowing. Hester's potatoes, saved for seed, would be planted by the end of this month of March. So would the oats, with corn shortly after, and then the garden.

At first she wept as she gripped the plow handles worn smooth by her father's hands and those of her brothers who now carried muskets, but, as she walked where they often had, breathing the same ripening earth, she gradually felt as if they were with her, Father, Charlie, Thos—Dan, too, and she was a little comforted although her shoulders ached and her fingers pained.

This was her war, not only for food, but for the peaceful, ordered flow of life the way it had been before. As spring came on, she mourned the sheep and the lambs that should be frisking now on the slopes. No pinkish black-and-white piglets tumbled over Evalina and Patches. Heloise and Abelard would honk no more warnings or deftly pick bugs out of the strawberries.

Still, in the valley, Moses and Pharaoh were safe, and Bess, Goldie, Clover, and Shadow had knobby-legged, big-eared calves at their sides. Her mother's surviving Wyandottes had hatched out adorable little fluff-balls. And there were the human babies, Noelle and Joely.

Christy sighed and confronted the truth. Melissa was not cheered by the lengthening, brighter days, the quickening of new life. She scarcely ate. Her milk seemed to give Joely colic, but she refused to permit Lilah to suckle him.

When Christy and Sarah had gone to the valley for the horses—*Where were Jed and Queenie? Pray God they fared well.*—her mother had taken Christy aside.

"I'm terribly worried about Melissa." Ellen herself was thin, but her color was good. And although there was an underlying sadness in her eyes, she enjoyed the other women's company, mothered Lilah, and often laughed, especially with the children. "Even Joely can't rouse her out of this soul-sickness," she had told Christy.

"She could go to Parkses'."

"That won't serve. She longs for her sister . . . her accustomed life."

Christy's heart sank but, indeed, watching her sister-in-law's prolonged despondency had made her fear the perilous journey to Sedalia would be necessary. "We'll plow and plant the potatoes," she said. "Then I'll borrow a wagon from the Parkses . . . some money, too, I'm afraid . . . and take Melissa to where she can get the train. Phronie will want to go with her, I'm sure."

Melissa had flushed at the news and thrown her arms around her mother-in-law. "Oh, Mama Ware! I can really go?" Then she had drooped and shook her head. "No. It's not fair to make Christy run such a risk." Her mouth quivered and she turned away.

Forcing down her resentment and misgivings, Christy had embraced this girl her brother loved. "Listen, dear, it's not your fault you can't like living in a cave, or even the long house Star's going to build. It's up to us to look after you and Joely since Charlie can't. You just eat and sleep so you'll be ready to travel in a week or so if the weather's decent."

So now Christy finished plowing the field, unharnessed the horses, rubbed them down, and treated them to dried persimmons. "I'm sorry there's no corn, you dear good ponies, but maybe Mister Parks will lend us a little so you won't get too gaunted-up on the way to Sedalia." She stood between the horses, running her fingers through their manes. They whuffed gently and nuzzled her. "I'm scared, ponies," she whispered. Lafe's taunting smile and chill eyes rose before her.

Again she heard the roar of Caxton's revolver, saw her father pitch forward. Trembling, she pressed her face to Lass's sweat-smelling, hard-muscled neck until grief and fear eased a little. "I hope we don't run into guerrillas or jayhawkers or just plain rascals. I hope I don't get you stolen away. Oh, Dan! I need you! I need someone!"

His last letter had said the Kansas regiments were being reorganized. Colonel Montgomery, sick of Lane's and Jennison's methods, had gone to Washington to seek a new command. Dan, Thos, and David would be serving with the 1st Kansas Battery. *I'm mighty tired of wrestling wagons through the snow and mud. Hope I can get assigned to a gun crew—and I hope we see some action. General Curtis's Union troops have chased Price out of Springfield and driven Old Pap Price and McCulloch, both, into the Boston Mountains down in Arkansas. Jeff Davis figured out a slick way to handle the trouble between McCulloch and Price. Instead of placing either in top command, he's formed the Trans-Mississippi Department No. 2—which is them, Jeff Thompson's swamp rats, and Pike's four regiments of Indians. The whole shebang is under the orders of General Earl Van Dorn, who will have about 45,000 men to Curtis's less than 11,000. The Confederates may not be able or willing to fight for a divided border state like Missouri, but they have to defend Arkansas. The 7th Kansas has been ordered out of Missouri to Humboldt, Kansas, a good forty-five miles west of the border—too far for quick forays across the state line. Anthony's cracked down on them hard—no more stealing pigs and chickens and cider. He's keeping them busy with three hours of company drill every morning and two hours of battalion and regimental drill in the afternoon. As you might suspect, quite a few men deserted who'd rather loot and burn, than learn to be soldiers.*

And then there were the dear words, sweet words, that

she read till she knew them by heart. She kept Dan's letters in the cherry-wood box her father had made for her. Ten of them, treasured and read over and over. Her mother had saved the two they'd had from Thos. *Would he be angry that they hadn't told him about Father and the raid? Yet what use was it to upset him when the plain truth was he might not live to come home, might never have to know what had happened?*

Her despairing wail to Dan faded as she thought of how lucky she was to be able to get his letters when nothing was heard from her brother Charlie or Travis Jardine. If they lived—how dreadful to always have to add that!—they must have been with Price in the retreat to the Arkansas mountains. God keep them.

The plea turned to driest ashes in her mouth. How many women were imploring God to save sons, brothers, husbands, or sweethearts who fought on different sides and would have to try to kill each other if they met? Still, she prayed.

Simeon Parks cheerfully loaned what should have been more than enough cash for Melissa's fare. "Better to have some extra than need it and not have it," he said. "You really should let Owen drive. . . ."

"We've been over that, Mister Parks. It's safer for me." She had a cup of sassafras tea with the women, and one of Catriona McHugh's scones, while watching red-headed little Andy and fair-haired Danny, both sixteen months old now, play with the wooden train Dan and Davie had carved and sent for Christmas.

"I'll bring the wagon back as soon as I can," she promised, returning the farewell embraces of Simeon's two daughters, Lydia and Susie, and his daughter-in-law, Harriet.

It was noon before Christy reached the home. She hid the wagon near a thicket of serviceberry, not yet leafed out but lovely with clustered white flowers, and turned the horses loose before going to the valley. Along with Robbie, Beth and Richie ran to meet her as she descended the rocks. "Come see Bob White!" called Beth.

"And . . . and Bobble!" shouted Richie.

Christy knelt to halt the hurtling little bodies with hers. They scrambled free after tumultuous hugs and kisses.

In the five days or so since she'd been gone, spring had quickened Peace Valley. Budding leaves were a mist of freshest green against dark cedar, white sycamore trunks, and the grays, browns, and silvers of the tribes of hickories, oaks, and maples. Some dogwoods were in flower, especially beautifully neighbored by blossoming redbuds or the fragrant yellow flowers of spicebush.

Brighter than spicebush blooms were male goldfinches shedding drab winter garb for bright yellow courting suits smartened with black wings, tail, and cap. Over the *jug-a-rum* of bullfrogs, red-winged blackbirds sang from the cat-tails and willows by the pond. Chickadees made two-noted nesting music, the first sound higher than the last, quite different from their usual namesake greetings. From everywhere—pond, river, meadow, cliffs, and woodlands—winged and chorused a celebration of birds while in the pale blue sky a wavey skein of geese called on their journey north.

Among the trees, Star, Hildy, Sarah, Lilah, and Ellen were collecting bark for the winter lodge. The loop of Noelle's cradleboard was hooked over the stob of a broken limb. In her third month now, the baby watched the women with curious brown eyes as the breeze tinkled the bells attached to the hide canopy and swayed the blue and scarlet feathers.

Christy proffered a finger. Creamy gold fingers gripped

it; the tiny nose scrunched as the baby gurgled and squealed. *Poor Joely, inside the cave with his brooding mother on a day like this that smelled and glowed and sang! Well, since Melissa hated it here, he'd be better off in Saint Louis. But look at Richie, not missing his big house and fine toys, full of glee as an otter pup, secure with his "aunts".*

When Christy spent a night in the cave, Beth still sometimes cried in her arms for her father, for murdered sheep and pigs, geese and chickens, for stolen Queenie and Jed— for Thos and Charlie and Dan. Yet most of the time, Christy had never seen Beth happier—protector and chief of Richie, with two babies to fuss over.

The mothering group of kind, capable women stopped their work to greet Christy.

She told them she had the wagon and money and wanted to leave as early as possible in the morning. Ellen took her daughter's hands and looked into her eyes in a way that sent Christy's heart thudding.

"My dear," said her mother, "I'm going, too."

"You mean you'll help Melissa and Joely get to Saint Louis?"

"Yes, but when they're safe at her sister's, I'm going to be a nurse."

"A nurse?"

Ellen nodded. "Should my sons, or Dan, or Travis, or young Davie Parks be wounded, I pray they'll be well cared for, but, from what we hear, the wounded lie untended for hours on a battlefield and then are tossed into any kind of wagon and jolted to filthy makeshift hospitals." She paused to get control of her voice. "How can I hope some other woman will give our boys a cool drink, help them eat, wash off blood and dirt, or soothe a fever, if I'm not willing to go and do what I can?"

Christy hadn't even thought of such a course. Now, compelled to, she tightened her hold on her mother's hands. "Mother, you can't do that! I . . . I'll go! Beth needs you."

Ellen freed one hand and smiled as she caressed Christy's cheek. "Bless you, I know you would, but I'm sure the nursing organizations wouldn't accept a young, unmarried woman. Besides, it's your staying that makes it possible for me to leave Beth." She glanced at the circle of women with gratitude. "Of course, I wouldn't go if these kind and caring friends hadn't agreed to look after Beth, but, even so, I couldn't leave her if you weren't here."

"But. . . ."

"Also, I'll probably be in and out of Saint Louis and can see Melissa and Joely often. I'd like to do that for Charlie's sake as well as my own." Ellen took Christy's face between her hands. "Please believe me, love. I need to do this. Just as you need to plow and plant and hold our land."

For the first time in her eighteen years, Christy saw her mother as separate from that identity, a woman with unsuspected depths and feelings, who had lost the husband who had also been her lover, who knew the agony of having sons on different sides in this war. Small wonder she was driven to throw herself into the relief of suffering men.

"Father would be proud of you." Christy spoke through aching tightness in her throat. "So would Thos and Charlie . . . and Dan and Travis." She brought her mother's hand to her lips and wet them with her tears. "So am I."

It was overcast next morning with a dull glitter of frost on the ground. Their chances of making the long journey in March without being rained or snowed on were slight, yet Christy had hoped for fair weather at the start and few uncomfortable nights of soaked featherbeds. The jayhawkers, not to mention guerrillas, had spent the winter pillaging and burning the region the women must travel through, although at least, thank goodness, Jennison's and Anthony's 7th Kansas was no longer marauding. The travelers couldn't count on the hospitality that had been the rule before the war; indeed, they'd be lucky if the wagon and horses weren't stolen. Christy only hoped, if that happened, it would be after her mother and Melissa were safely on the train.

Ellen hated the thought of Christy's driving back alone, and Sarah had offered to come, but any extra burdening of the horses seemed cruel. "If I don't meet bad people, there won't be any danger," Christy argued. "If I do, there'd be one more person in trouble."

"Your father and brothers would. . . ."

"Not worry half as much as if they knew what you intend to do, Mother!"

That forced a grudging laugh from Ellen. Now, preparing for the journey, Christy spread the wagon bed with the heavy canvas that had covered their wagon on the way from Illinois, left over half of it trailing, and heaped featherbeds, quilts, and blankets to make a resting place. She filled a Dutch oven with coals, covered them with ashes, and set the iron pot in a big cast-iron skillet beneath the wagon seat, securing them with boxes of food. These were buttressed with sacks of oats and corn Simeon Parks had given her for the horses who'd have little time to graze even if the grass were more than a green shadow here and there. She flipped the loose canvas over the bedding. If it stormed, everyone but the driver could shelter under the cloth.

Taking their halters and a pocketful of oats, she went to get Lad and Lass who enjoyed their treat and nuzzled her as she led them toward the hazel thicket. She almost had them harnessed when Melissa came up with Joely in her arms and a grumbling Emmie on her back in a rush basket contrived to leave only her gray head free. Ellen and Phronie followed, cumbered with bundles carried in rawhide slings and fastened to their backs.

The softer belongings served as pillows. The others were stowed wherever they fitted best. Emmie's carrier was cunning, indeed. Set lengthwise, it was a comfortable lodging for the cat. Star had contrived it to close with thongs, and lined it with woven rushes that could be cleaned out as necessary.

"She was nice enough not to remind me that I wouldn't put Joely in the cradleboard," Melissa confessed. A spark of the old playfulness was back in her deep blue eyes. "I wish now I'd used it. Think how amazed my sister's friends would be!"

Christy took her place on the blanket-padded seat while Phronie scrambled up beside her. "Bless God and you, child," she muttered. "I'm almighty thankful to be out of the cave! But it served its turn, it surely did."

Christy hoped Lad and Lass's shoes would last out the journey. With Andy McHugh gone, they hadn't been shod that spring. Their hoofs needed trimming and the old shoes were wearing thin. If there was money left after train fares, she'd find a blacksmith in Sedalia.

They didn't stop at the Hayeses' tannery, but forded the creek and took the rutted road to Butler, the county seat. Allie Hayes wouldn't willingly cause them trouble, but the less people noticed them, the better.

"How far to that train, Miss Christy?" Nothing would induce Phronie to drop the "Miss" although Lilah and Hildy did now without embarrassment.

"Over a hundred miles. It'll probably take us four or five days."

They passed the turn-off to Lige and Sarah Morrow's and shortly after rumbled past the Franzes' abandoned house. The apple tree where Emil had been hung was budding, but the grapevines were still bare gnarls. The log in the orchard still protected the grave Hester had dug for Emil and Lottie. When there was time, time to do more than just stay alive, Christy resolved to bring Lass over and haul a big stone beside the log, chisel on it the Franzes' names and day of death.

Shingles had blown off the Barclay cabin's roof and it was almost overgrown with vines. "I hope the family's doing well back in Ohio," Ellen said. "Tressie and Phyllis were bright, sweet little girls."

How long ago those school days seemed, thought Christy. To think that five years ago Lafe Ballard had studied across the table from her! Now Matthew and Mark Hayes might have to fight Thos, their schoolmate. And the man who had made ancient times and far places seem real to the children, who had taught with laughter and love, was now returning to the earth at the edge of his field.

They stopped at noon near a little creek. Christy unharnessed Lad and Lass, let them go to water, and then put grain in their nosebags. Walking around to stretch their cramped bodies, the women ate sliced raw turnip, cold oat cakes, and finished with nibbles of the dark maple sugar Star had given Melissa as a gift to her sister. When the horses had rested a while, Christy hitched them up, and the party traveled on.

The sky overhead darkened even more. Christy glanced up at the teeming clouds that shadowed the land as far as the eye could reach. Suddenly the mass descended, glimmering giant veils of blue and gray, dropping through distant trees to feed on acorns left from their autumn foraging.

"Passenger pigeons!" Phronie sighed. "Nothing tastier than a mess of squab cooked in butter."

Some would nest deeply in the woods but most would gorge and fly on northward as they had done time out of mind. To see them pursue their age-old rhythms in spite of human woes strengthened Christy. That was good, for as the road left the trees for rolling prairie, they began to pass what had been farms and was now wasteland—straggles of rail fence that the jayhawkers hadn't used to roast stolen cattle, pigs, and fowl; charred stubs of logs amid toppled foundation stones; heaps of hide and bone from hastily butchered cattle, but not a living farm animal except a blind old horse with skeleton ribs and a white cow that had eluded capture and now wandered with her calf.

Christy stopped, gave Phronie the reins, and put oats and corn in her skirt. Calling softly to the horse, she dropped the grain in easy reach. "Poor creatures!" Ellen said as Christy got back on the seat. "Why do they suffer for our quarrels?"

There was no answer to that, or the ruin brought to families who had once lived in homes marked only by blackened débris and chimneys thrusting up like elongated tombstones. "Jennison's monuments" they were called, although most likely some of the farms had belonged to Union folk driven out by Secessionist neighbors when it seemed Price would reclaim the state.

"Nothing but chimneys," Phronie groaned. "Same as at Rose Haven!"

Dusk was falling when they came in sight of what had to be Butler since there were no other towns anywhere close. The hopeful little town, barely settled, had just been made the county seat when the Wares passed through almost six years ago. Now lamps or fires glowed dimly from a few houses scattered forlornly around the burned courthouse, businesses, and torched dwellings.

"Shall we ask to spend the night with someone?" Christy asked.

"No." Her mother's voice shook. "I . . . I'd rather sleep in the wagon. Even if it rains."

Although dogs barked and raced beside the wagon, not a soul opened a door or appeared in a window. Christy drove past the charcoal shards of the courthouse to halt a mile out of town in a fringe of trees along a stream.

While she hobbled, rubbed down, and grained the horses, Ellen scooped out a hollow for the coals from the Dutch oven. Soon a crackling fire warmed them, heated the skillet of hominy seasoned with butter, and boiled water in the coffee pot to brew spicewood tea.

Joely whimpered at the strangeness, but Melissa's milk apparently agreed with him now, because, after nursing hungrily, he fell asleep. Phronie took him to bed in the wagon, curling her slight frame at one end to make room for Melissa and Ellen.

After the coals were banked against the morning, Christy took off her dress, put it under the canvas, and got the oldest blanket and quilt. Mantling these around her, she crawled under the wagon, arranged the bedding as comfortably and warmly as she could, and fell asleep to the "who-cooks-for-you-who-cooks-for-you-all?" of a barred owl.

CHAPTER SIX

Only one house stood in Dayton among over forty burned ones. "I can't imagine anyone could be very glad to have their house spared when all their neighbors' were burned." Her mother's words were Christy's thoughts. This was the town Daniel Anthony had destroyed on New Year's Day two months ago.

"I wonder where everyone's gone?" Melissa held Joely closely as she peered around.

"It'd be no marvel if the men joined the guerrillas." Christy's voice stuck in her throat. "Some families probably moved far enough east to be out of reach of the jayhawkers."

"It's a dirty, dirty war!" Melissa cried. "Lincoln's a long-jawed ape, but I'd think even he wouldn't want robbing murderers in the U.S. uniform!"

"I don't think any of the regular Union officers like the way Jennison and Lane have behaved in Missouri," Ellen said. "They've been ordered far enough into Kansas to stop their looting."

Melissa curled her lip. "After there's not much left!"

"The Seventh Kansas will probably get sent a long way from the border," Christy guessed. "But that'll give the guerrillas a freer hand, and they're certainly no better than the jayhawkers."

With grain and several hours of rest at noon, Lad and Lass were holding up well. Christy and her mother took advantage of the halts to gather young cat-tails, wild greens, and onions, welcome additions to their food. Cloudy skies threatened and thunder reverberated after distant zigzags of lightning, but, to the travelers' relief, the storms spent their fury elsewhere. It rained the second night, but not enough to penetrate the canvas.

There were no towns between Dayton and Sedalia and only sooted chimneys remained of the few farmhouses they passed. Except for the shadows glimpsed through windows in Butler, they had not seen a single human being.

"It's as if we're the only people left," Melissa said in a frightened tone.

Ellen touched her hand. "There'll be plenty of folks in Sedalia . . . and Saint Louis must be overflowing with people, from both sides, seeking refuge."

"Oh, I hope the city hasn't turned horrid!"

"There hasn't been any trouble there since General Lyon took the armory," soothed Ellen. "Gracious, that seems so long ago, but it's really less than a year!"

"Yes." Melissa's tone was bitter. "Charlie and Travis rode off like knights of the round table, and we all thought the war would be over by autumn."

Thos went, too. Christy thought of her brother. *And Dan, Owen, and Andy . . . Andy, who'll never come back to Susie and his little son . . . Andy, buried with John Brown's testament under the roots of a blasted tree at Wilson's Creek.*

"My mother's dead and my father's murdered," Melissa went on. "Rose Haven's gone. Papa Ware was such a good man, and he's killed, too!" Melissa's voice caught on a sob. She buried her face against Ellen's shoulder. "Oh, Mama Ware, I can't bear it . . . I can't . . . if Charlie and Travis don't come back!"

Ellen held her close. "We have to pray they will, my dear."

Christy swallowed and rubbed an arm across her eyes.

Then she rubbed them again, unwilling to believe what she saw. Trees followed a creek perhaps half a mile away. Christy had just been planning to stop there for the night. Now, out of the trees rode a dozen men or more.

Phronie moaned. "Oh, Lord, have mercy!"

Melissa screamed.

"Hush!" warned Ellen. "Melissa, you and Phronie get under the canvas with Joely. I've got the butcher knife. But remember . . . so far, neither side's hurt women on purpose."

No use hoping the riders lazily closing the distance between them could be anything but jayhawks—those were by no means limited to Jennison's uniformed ones—or, more likely, guerrillas or downright thieves. There was little to choose between the species.

"If they try to bother us, Phronie, grab the shovel and hit anyone you can reach." Christy's mouth was dry. "I'll toss the coals at them and hit them with the lid."

None of this would do much good if the men meant serious harm, but chances were they'd ride on when they saw no men were with the women and there was nothing worth stealing—except, oh, my God! The fare money!

"Mother," called Christy softly, "put the money at the bottom of the diaper bucket."

Ellen actually laughed. "What a wonderful notion! If I know men, a sniff of the bucket is all they'll want."

The leader rode a big bay, not Bill Anderson's handsome black, but perhaps he'd be a friend of Bill's—or at least afraid of him. The horsemen moved like part of the gathering dusk, the hoofs of their mounts muffled by new grass and sere tufts of last year's. Christy could now see their plumed hats and bright guerrilla shirts, red and blue, embroidered and beaded, although a few wore fringed buckskins.

Something about the man on the bay. . . . His dark hat

with a flowing black plume shadowed his face, but she could tell he wasn't Bill Anderson. Mounted on mettlesome horses that were clean-limbed and deep-chested, the guerrillas ranged in front of Lad and Lass, forcing them to stop. At most of the bridles hung what looked like wigs, some of them long. The band carried rifles or shotguns and each man bristled with revolvers, some carrying half a dozen in holsters or thrust through belts. Clumsy, beef-shouldered Tom Maddux was the only one Christy knew—till the leader swept off his hat.

Lafe Ballard chuckled at her instinctive shrinking. "Miss Christy, Miz Ware, what a delight to meet with neighbors! But I do hope you're not leaving the country."

"We're bound for Sedalia." Ellen tried to keep her tone pleasant. "I'm going to visit my daughter-in-law in Saint Louis."

One bleached eyebrow lifted towards silvery hair. "Miss Jardine . . . beg pardon . . . young Miz Ware's gone to the city? I heard what the confounded jayhawks did to Rose Haven."

"It's natural that she wished to join her sister, though we miss her, of course."

"Of course."

Could he say anything that didn't sound mocking? Christy thought, before she said: "We should move on." She lifted the reins. "We need to make camp before nightfall."

"Allow me to invite you to stop near our camp in the trees across the ford. A lop-eared Dutch farmer compelled us to take a pig and fine turkey that are cooking on spits over our fire. You're welcome to share."

"Thank you. We have our own food." Christy's mind whirred desperately. These men would surely not hurt Melissa and the baby, ardent Southerner that Melissa's father, the bishop, had been, but they might well seize Phronie and sell her. And some man might brave the smell of the diaper bucket.

"At least accept our protection." Lafe's teeth flashed. "I insist!"

"Cap'n!" bawled Tom Maddux. "Somethin' be wigglin' under the tarp!"

"You'll excuse us if we satisfy Tom's curiosity?" Lafe drawled.

"My dear boy. . . ," Ellen began.

He raised a peremptory hand. "I was never your dear boy, madam. Endured with a smile, yes, because of your soft-brained Universalist nonsense, but let's not pretend that had it not been for my mother, your husband would have expelled me long before I took myself off."

"Your mother's well. . . ."

"I supposed she would be." His voice was indifferent. "All right, Tom. Let's see what's under that canvas. Have your pistols handy, men. These ladies are for the Union. Might have a jayhawk tucked away."

Melissa threw back the cover and sat up with blazing eyes, Joely clasped so tight he howled. She did have the presence of mind to leave Phronie hidden. "I'm no jayhawk, Lafe Ballard! You ought to be ashamed of yourself, skulking around stealing pigs and turkeys and plaguing women, instead of fighting with General Price like my brother and my husband . . . Mama Ware's son, remember!"

"To be sure, Charlie and Travis have doubtless run valiantly with Price all the way to the Boston Mountains. Never mind. They may be fighting this very minute at Pea Ridge, just over the border in Arkansas." Lafe scratched his head in mock puzzlement. "Now how is it your mother-in-law's traveling to visit you in Saint Louis, Miz Ware, when you're right here?" He shook his head and looked sorrowfully at Ellen. "I'm afraid your husband would be disappointed, madam, to hear you lie so glib."

"We are going to Saint Louis!" Melissa's cheeks were furious red. "I'm going to my sister whose husband is in the real Army!"

"Yes," murmured Lafe. "The real Army that cares not a fig for Missouri and abandons it to the likes of Jennison and Lane. These are hard times, yet I can scarce believe, Miz Jardine-Ware, that the young mistress of Rose Haven is traveling without at least one servant."

Phronie rose up, put a protective arm around her nursling. "I be here where I belong, Master Lafe, but you, you sure not where you ought to be!"

"The wagon's full of surprises." Lafe grinned and gestured to his men. "Have a look in the bedding and bundles, but first help the ladies down."

Ignoring the brigands' offered hands, the women got down. Christy, soothing Lad and Lass, didn't try to smother a laugh when Tom Maddux yelped and dropped the hot lid of the Dutch oven. No one, thank goodness, explored the contents of the diaper bucket.

"Nothin' worth havin', Cap'n, 'cept this maple sugar," growled a man with a tangled red beard.

"That's for my sister!" protested Melissa.

"As fine a Confederate lady as she must be, she won't grudge it to defenders of the cause." Lafe's indulgent manner changed. His pale eyes narrowed, reflecting the dying light. "You must have money for train fare. Kindly let us have it."

"I must ask the Union commander in Sedalia to pay our passage."

"For the wife and mother of a Rebel soldier?"

"For the wife of a murdered Union man and the mother of a Union soldier."

"How differently that rings! Yet I trust you won't blame me, Miz Ware, for not quite believing you after the way you've endeavored to deceive me. I'm afraid I must ask you to yield up the money or be searched, shameful and distressing as that will be."

Ellen stiffened but held her tongue. With an effort, so did Christy. What could they do? Resisting would only lead to violent manhandling, possibly even worse.

Tom Maddux, grinning, turned toward Melissa.

"Don't touch me!" she hissed. "The money's in the bottom of the diaper pail. Have a good time finding it!"

"Reckon we won't do that." Lafe stared at Phronie. "I remember how you never let me eat in the kitchen at Rose Haven. Sent me out in the yard. All right, you old yellow hag, fish the coins out for us. Don't try to hold back any. We'll dump the bucket just to make sure."

"You was snot-nosed then, you be snot-nosed now, and that's the way you'll die." Phronie's green eyes shone like a cat's. "I'd sooner wade up to my neck in a baby's mess than touch ary one of you with a ten-foot pole."

"Wonder how much we can get for the old nigger," Lafe said to the red-beard who was munching some of the maple sugar he'd handed around. "Might bring a better price without that sassy tongue."

"White trash you be, Lafe Ballard. Never had the price of a one-eyed gaboon in your pocket! You. . . ."

"Aunt Phronie!" Melissa begged, tugging at her. "Get them the money."

Phronie rolled up her sleeves, reached through the diapers soaking in soft soap and water, and tossed coins out on the turf. They winked silver and gold. "That be all."

"We'll see. Dump the bucket," Lafe instructed one of the men.

Phronie stooped, gripped the handle, straightened, and, as she did so, tossed diapers and sudsy water all over Lafe.

"Oh, Phronie!" wailed Ellen.

One yellow-splotched diaper dangled from Lafe's plumed hat. Another festooned a shoulder. More lay about his boots.

Horrified as she was, Christy couldn't keep from laughing. Nor could Lafe's men.

"Got you right smart, Cap'n!" chortled Red Beard, doubling with hilarity. "Good God A'mighty, when Quantrill hears about this . . . !"

"He better not hear." Lafe shook off the smelly encumbrances and stepped out of the puddle. A revolver flashed in either hand. "Now, gentlemen, if anyone still thinks it's funny, here's his chance to die laughing."

There was instant sobriety. "Aw, Lafe!" whined ungainly Tom Maddux.

Christy put herself in front of Phronie, who did not flinch at the pistols. "Haven't you heard that Bill Anderson . . . who was left at our house . . . will come after anyone who bothers us?"

"Ah, yes, Bill. Gets a trifle above himself sometimes." Lafe moved to where he could pin Phronie with his eyes.

She didn't cringe, but after a moment she shivered.

Lafe smiled. "You want me to kill you, don't you, you old yellow whore?"

Phronie didn't answer, only glared at him like a small, cornered beast. He shoved Christy out of the way and slapped Phronie so hard she staggered against the wagon. Blood oozed from a split lip.

"Don't want to be sold away from your mistress? Answer

me, bitch, or I'll cut off that curly hair of hers and tie it to my bridle."

"Rather I die than leave my Miss Melissa."

"You won't get what you want."

"What you mean?"

"If you're alive, when we get through with you, we'll sell you for whatever we can get." Lafe shrugged. "If you're dead, we'll toss you to the first hogs we come across."

Ellen laid her hand on his arm. "Lafe, you don't mean it! You can't hurt an old woman like Phronie!" He didn't step back from her hand, but, at his stare, Ellen drew away her fingers as if they'd touched corruption.

"I can do anything I want to her, Miz Ware." Lafe's tone was soft as his gaze swept over them, stopping at Christy. "*Anything* I want. To *any* of you. As far as you're concerned, I'm the devil and God Almighty rolled into one."

Tom Maddux stirred uncomfortably. "Now, Lafe, Cap'n, do whatever you want with the old nigger, but we ain't hurtin' white ladies, 'less they pull guns or knives on us."

"Still, it may edify them to know what we'll do with the hag," Lafe mused, then chuckled. "Rather wade in baby shit than touch us, would you? Well, we can have some good of you, first. It'll soon be so dark we can't see your ugly face. While the boys wait their turn, they can be filling up a trench with piss and shit. You can have a nice soak in it when we're finished. If you don't drown or choke, we'll souse you in the creek and sell you to the first one who'll have you."

"You can't do that!" Melissa placed Joely in the wagon bed and threw her arms around Phronie. "You'll have to kill me first!"

Ellen took the butcher knife from under her shawl.

"You'll have to kill us all."

"Aw, Lafe," muttered Red Beard. "Cain't we jist . . . ?"

Christy said: "Lafe, I want to talk to you. Please."

"Now that's a word I thought never to hear from you, Miss Christy." He smiled into her eyes, his own like frost. "Indeed, I like the sound."

"Please."

He offered his arm. "Shall we have a stroll, then?"

"Christy!" called Ellen. "Don't . . . !" Her voice broke off as if she didn't know what to ask Christy not to do.

Christy slipped her hand as loosely as possible through Lafe's bent arm, but he caught her fingers in a grip cold and hard as steel. "So, Christy?"

"Don't hurt Phronie. I'm begging you."

"Beg harder."

"How?"

"Make me an offer."

"You have our money, borrowed, at that. Take the horses."

He shook his head. "That's not enough to save that yellow hide."

Christy's blood chilled, then thundered in her ears. She could barely whisper. "What is?"

"You."

Her heart beat like the wings of a caged hawk. "Now?"

"No. It's not the time or place for what I've dreamed about." He laughed at her start of surprise. "Don't think I love you. It's not that." He lifted her wrist, kissed the scar he'd made there when they were children. "You're the one I think about when I do things to girls. More than being my first woman, you're the first I hurt."

It was like looking into a slimy, stinking pit that crawled with eyeless monsters. Christy tried to take her hand away.

He held it in that steel grasp, a thumb splayed on the scar over the pulse of her blood.

"Let me visit you." He laughed as her imprisoned hand convulsed. "It may take only a few days and nights. Usually a single night gives me a disgust of any woman I've wanted."

She was in the pit, fondled by obscene creatures, mired in their filth. *Dan, how can you love me if that happens? How can I stand myself?* "Let Phronie alone, let her stay with us . . . and I'll open the door to you."

"And yourself?"

"Yes."

"I won't burn you again." His voice was husky. "That was the crude work of a boy. I know better ways now, Christy, to put my mark on you."

"How Hester can have a son like you. . . ."

"I had a daddy, too. Used to go at Ma even in daylight. Shut me out of the cabin, but I watched through the chinks." Lafe chuckled at Christy's sound of abhorrence. "Ma thought he stumbled and fell on the scythe, although he'd sure have had to fall at a peculiar angle to get the blade in his neck like that."

"You did it?"

"I wanted to have Ma to myself." A dismissive shrug. "No more locked doors. Guess what? Once I got her attention, I didn't want her."

At Christy's shocked silence, he laughed and let his long cold fingers trail down her face from temple to throat. "What a dirty mind you have! I never wanted Ma that way. I just didn't like her studying to please that man, instead of looking after me."

"Let's go back," Christy suggested.

He turned obligingly. "I know what you're thinking."

"Do you?"

"You think you'll open the door to me, but you'll kill me if you can."

"That shouldn't be too hard."

"You may be surprised." He paused. In a voice like silk, he spoke dreamily: "The best time I ever had with a woman, Christy, was with one I choked to death. She bucked and fought . . . emptied me out clear down to my toes."

Christy refused to allow herself to tremble. "Maybe we'll both be surprised."

"I'm sure of that." Laughter came from so deep in his throat it was almost a growl. "So we have our bargain. The old wench stays with her mistress, and you'll unbar your door. I'll be delayed, I fear. My band's joining Quantrill for some important action, but I suspect you can control your impatience."

"Will you give us back the train fare?"

"We need it to buy cartridges to protect Missouri." At her derisive laugh, he added: "Doubtless we'll buy some whiskey, too. Be grateful I'll leave you the horses and wagon."

"Oh, I am," she said sarcastically, but with truth. "Very, very grateful."

He released her only after they reached the shadowy group near the wagon, but it was so dark that she didn't think anyone could see her hand had been in his. "Let's get back to camp, boys!" Lafe called.

No one argued. It could be some of them would have vented their lust on Phronie, but probably not even they had any stomach for the whole of Lafe's plan.

"You're still welcome to share our supper," Lafe told the women mockingly.

"I think we'll get a little farther down the road," Christy

said, glancing at the fires flickering through the trees across the creek. She wished they were the flames of hell, waiting to embrace Lafe Ballard. One thing sure: she'd never tell Hester about this encounter, much less the pact she'd made, a promise to the devil. To her mother's and Melissa's anxious queries, she only said she'd talked to Lafe of their childhood and of his mother.

"We must pray for him . . . for Hester's sake," said Ellen.

"I pray for him!" Phronie's words were distorted by her swollen lips. "Pray he burn infernal and eternal!"

Ellen didn't chide her, but said with a surprising twinkle: "You ought to think instead, Phronie, of how droll he looked with a diaper hanging from his plume."

Phronie cackled. "Oh, I'll study on that, Miss Ellen!" She added darkly: "I'll get the shivers to my dyin' day when I remember how he looked at me with those blue-john eyes and said what-all he aimed to do with me! I hoped I could make him mad enough to shoot me in the head."

"Thank God, he didn't!" shuddered Melissa. "Don't you pull such a trick again, Aunt Phronie! If you got sold away, I'd get you back."

"Lord, child, I know you'd try, you and Miss Yvonne. But in this war, where everything's turned topsy-turvy and upside down, who knows what's gonna happen?" She giggled as she took Joely. "Won't it a be story to tell him, how his didies hid gold coins and got tossed all over a fire-breathin', cock-struttin' guerrilla?"

By the time they got to Sedalia, Lad had lost two shoes and Lass one. Since they had to throw themselves on the mercy of the post commander, Christy hoped he might tell a military farrier to shoe the team. Sedalia thrived from the railroad and being one of the major Federal military posts on the eastern boundary of what amounted to a guerrilla-haunted no man's land now that the 7th Kansas had been ordered well over the state line.

Christy halted the team near the railway station to hear what the jubilation was about. It didn't take long to learn that the Union had won a decisive victory at Pea Ridge two days ago, March 8th, after a day and a half of battle.

"They're calling General Price 'Old Skedad'!"

A just-arrived train passenger waved a St. Joseph paper. "Editor says as a racer he's got few equals for his weight . . . he weighs close to three-hundred pounds, you know! Pity the horse that has to tote him!"

Glancing from her mother to Melissa and Phronie, Christy knew they all had the same thought. Had Charlie and Travis lived to skedaddle? That anxiety, along with the certainty that countless men on both sides were dead or maimed for life, blunted Christy's relief that the Union had won. Melissa, of course, looked devastated.

"Pike's Choctaws took scalps," growled a soldier.

"Yes," countered a citizen who looked anything but joyful. He must have been one of the few Secessionists left in town. "And Sigel's lop-eared Dutchmen butchered surrendered Confederates! We know Sigel, damn him, he was in command of a division here after he ran away at Wilson's Creek! Some might call murdering unarmed prisoners worse than scalping dead enemies."

"Who says they were all dead?" bristled the soldier. "Some wounded had their skulls split by Bowie knives before the hair was ripped off."

A blond, young captain stepped casually between the angry men. "You've got to credit Van Dorn for guts," he said. "He was sick and still not recovered from a bad fall from his horse, but he commanded from an ambulance."

"That may be," granted the man with the paper. "But he had between sixteen thousand and twenty-five thousand men against Curtis's ten thousand five hundred. Curtis reports almost fourteen hundred killed, wounded, or missing. There's no telling how many Van Dorn really lost, because they deserted in droves after the battle. He admits to a thousand, with three hundred more taken prisoner."

"He's making for east of the Mississippi where a battle's shaping up at a place called Shiloh," put in the captain. "Van Dorn needs to win back his reputation. Pike and his Indians headed back to Indian Territory, but Price will follow Van Dorn. Pea Ridge had to prove, even to Pap Price, that he can't regain Missouri without a lot more help than the Confederacy has given him so far. Maybe he hopes, if his Missourians fight hard in the East, other troops will eventually be put under his command for a fresh attempt." He shook his head with considerable sympathy. "Poor old Pap! In spite of the luck he's had, he just can't believe there aren't enough Secesh in Missouri to flock to his banner and run out our Federal troops!"

"At least Ben McCulloch won't give him any more trouble." The soldier grinned. "Killed in battle the first day. Someone stole his weapons and gold watch, but they left him his fancy Wellington boots. Seems that only an hour after a carriage rattled into Fayetteville with his body, another rolled in with General McIntosh."

"Brave generals, both of them," said the captain with respectful sadness. Noticing the women in the farm wagon, he came over, doffing his hat. "Is there any way I could serve you ladies? You seem to be traveling."

"Indeed, sir, we'd be much obliged if you'd escort us to your commanding officer," said Ellen Ware. "Guerrillas robbed us of our train fare. My daughter-in-law and I must go to Saint Louis, so we're hoping for assistance."

"I'm bound you'll get it, ma'am. Just follow me."

On hearing their story, the colonel scowled. "This happened day before yesterday? There'll be no finding them, I'm afraid, but I'll send out a party. Like will-o'-the-wisps, these rascals! Bands of three or four hundred gather for a raid, and then melt into the countryside. After all, that's where they live, which makes this kind of war the very . . . I beg your pardon, ladies!"

He wrote passes for the three women, and insisted on lending them some cash they could repay to the company fund. He assigned the captain to help them on the train, and tried to persuade Christy to go with them.

"You'd be much safer in Saint Louis, my dear young lady." Instead of the fatherly-looking officer wearing his colonel's eagle on his shoulder straps, it was embroidered inside a gold-edged circle of infantry sky blue. "Surely you should remain with your mother."

Amazed that she hadn't considered going, despite the threat of Lafe's visit, Christy did try for a moment to imagine what she'd do in St. Louis, but, even if Beth hadn't been in the valley, she couldn't abandon their home, her father's fields and grave, the ground ready for planting, the hope of harvest.

"Thank you, sir," she told the major, "but I'm going home."

"I can't spare an escort."

"Sir, I'd never ask for one. Perhaps, though, my horses could be shod?"

After a regretful stare, he said: "Captain Hunt, after the other ladies are on the train, see that this young woman is provisioned, including grain for her horses, and make sure the horses are shod." He rose and bowed over the women's hands. "May God keep all of you."

The train huffed in from Jefferson City, disgorged passengers, and was hastily unloaded. While it took on wood and water, Christy and Captain Hunt helped Ellen, Melissa, and Phronie aboard. Joely howled at the commotion and strangeness, but the captain diverted him with a chunk of villainous flat bread he extracted from a pocket.

"Hard tack's just the thing to teeth on, ma'am," Hunt assured a dubious Melissa. Joely attacked it with gusto.

Christy kissed them all good bye, urging her mother to be careful, and begging them all to write.

As cinders flew and black smoke curled, they waved to each other till the train dipped out of sight. The captain offered Christy his reasonably clean handkerchief. "Miss Ware, while our farrier sees to your team, allow me to treat you to pie and coffee at the home of a widow who is of estimable character, although she profits madly from selling baked goods to soldiers."

The frank admiration in his merry blue eyes took away some of the dirty feeling Christy had since the encounter with Lafe Ballard. "You're very kind, Captain Hunt, but perhaps you should know that. . . ." She hesitated. It seemed presumptuous to warn him that she was engaged when doubtless he regarded the hospitality as part of his duty.

"Of course, you have a sweetheart, Miss Ware," he said with a wry laugh. "How could it be otherwise? Is he in the Army?"

"With the Third Kansas." Far be it from her to reveal Dan's despised job of driving mules!

"Then he won't grudge a fellow soldier the pleasure of a

103

few hours of your company." Hunt ordered a private to take the horses to the farrier and scrawled a note to the quartermaster for grain and food to be stowed in the wagon. That done, he offered Christy his arm, gilt eagle buttons at the cuff, and helped her across the muddy street.

In her gingham-curtained kitchen, on an oak table polished with beeswax, the Widow McNelly served them big chunks of dried peach pie with thick cream. There was more cream for the coffee, although, as she filled their ironstone cups, the pretty brown-haired woman apologized. "I can't get real coffee beans most of the time. The soldiers sell me their used ones. You'd think they might give them to me."

"I'm sure they would, dear lady, if you ever gave them a free piece of pie. Anyway, you charge them for the coffee they drink here, don't you?"

"Of course I do!" she said indignantly. "I have to earn my living!"

"Just so, ma'am." Captain Hunt smiled. "I'll tell my striker to bring you the part of my coffee ration I'm bound he's selling somewhere."

Christy had never flirted, but the captain was so adept at it that she found it fun and easy. Underneath her laughter and word play, though, she knew that somewhere beyond this protected town Lafe Ballard ranged at will, and many others like him.

Later, when Captain Hunt helped her into the wagon, he dropped his bantering gaiety. "It seems terrible to let you go like this, Miss Ware. I'm sure Missus McNelly would share her home with you if you'd stay on."

Christy took the reins and smiled with more cheer than she felt. "You're very good to care, sir, but I have crops and a garden to plant, a house to keep, and friends who expect me."

He closed his big hand over hers. "Then I can only beg you to be careful. And remember I'll always be very much at your service if . . . ," he floundered. "If you ever need me."

She knew he meant if Dan were killed, and was glad he hadn't said it. She returned the pressure of his fingers. "Thank you for everything, Captain. If you ever pass near my home, you'll be welcome."

"I'll remember." He stepped back.

Her hand, briefly comforted by the warmth of his, felt chilled and lonely. She started the team. The merry *chink* of their new shoes found no echo in her heart. Her mother was gone. That struck now with full force. Until her mother had gone to live in the valley, Christy had rarely been away from her for more than a few hours. Her mother expected her and the other women to look after Beth, but didn't she think Christy needed her, too?

Desolation welled up in Christy along with the angry hurt she'd managed to deny till then. With her father dead, it was too much to lose her mother, too! Tears slid down Christy's face. No matter how fiercely she blinked, she had to keep scrubbing them away.

Gradually she had to listen to an insistent voice. *Your mother didn't try to persuade you to go with her. She could have insisted you and Beth come to stay at Melissa's sister's, which would certainly have relieved her mind, but she knew how you feel about the house and farm. You can't know how she feels about losing her husband . . . having sons on different sides of this awful war. She's not just your mother, you selfish stupid! She's Ellen Ware.*

The sense of loss was still there, but self-pity withered. If only there were some way to know if Charlie and Travis had survived Pea Ridge, know where they were! Charlie didn't even know his baby was a son; he was missing these months when Joely constantly learned and changed. And Travis, how could he resist winsome little Noelle, who had his eyes and hair?

As Christy passed the last farms protected by closeness to the soldiers at Sedalia, Lafe's taunting face rose before her. What devilment would he be up to with Quantrill? She grimaced at the thought of their claiming to be patriots, defending Missouri. They certainly hadn't done much to keep Jennison's jayhawkers from burning towns and farms!

She hoped Lafe wouldn't live to visit her. If he did, at least he knew she'd try to kill him. What would be the price if she succeeded? As always when the quicksand of hate and grief swelled high and threatened to overwhelm her, Christy imagined being with Dan. She kissed his roughly tender mouth, the cruel marks on his cheek, rested her face against his heart. And heard him play his song.

CHAPTER SEVEN

While Kansas regiments reorganized that spring of 1862 at Leavenworth, Dan O'Brien and his friends gritted their teeth at delays as news came of distant battles. Charlie Ware and Travis Jardine had probably been with what was left of Pap Price's command, early in April, at the two-day battle of Shiloh in Tennessee where Grant had held fast. Neither side could claim victory, only count their losses, great as many whole armies were here in the West—13,000 Union soldiers, 10,000 Confederates. A week later, Nashville fell, the first Confederate state capital to be vanquished. By the end of that month, Admiral David Glasgow Farragut's fleet had taken New Orleans. Way out in New Mexico Territory, even, Confederates won battles at Val Verde and Tucson while the Union triumphed at Glorieta Pass.

After what seemed forever, Dan's group rolled out of Leavenworth in early June, part of a properly equipped battery. They finally had real uniforms, even if they were made of shoddy—a cheap cloth of reused fibers that must have made the contractors a fortune. Besides six, long-range, ten-pounder Parrotts of three-inch caliber with their caissons, the 1st Kansas Battery owned a forge, water wagon, a wagon with leather and harness repair supplies and tools, six wagons of camp gear, provender for men, mules, and horses, six ammunition wagons, and one ambulance. Dan thanked his stars that this time he rode Raven, instead of perching on the left-hand wheel mule to control one of the six-mule teams with a jerk line.

Soldiers who lived near the route were given brief furloughs, so Thos Ware and Dan were allowed to ride battery horses home. Dan stopped at the Parkses' mill just long enough to embrace Lydia and Susie—Uncle Simeon, too. Lydia fetched the resin for his violin bow, and he and Thos rode on to Wares'.

Is that Christy, Dan asked himself, *face hidden by a sunbonnet, using all her slender strength to hold the plow between the rows of green corn that reached to her knee?*

The bay started limping. The woman stopped the plow and waited in the field, till she recognized the two and ran forward, arms outstretched, bonnet flying from her hair—laughing, crying, calling their names. . . .

Dan's throat ached when Christy showed him Jonathan Ware's grave at the edge of that field. Thos knelt by the grassy mound and sobbed till Christy hugged him and said they must come with her to see Beth—and something wonderful.

Leading their horses, the men followed her through the cavern, flickering with the dance of her lantern light. Dan gasped at sight of the broad green valley, and, as they stared down, Beth and a golden-haired little boy ran to meet them.

Sarah, Star, and Hildy made them welcome while Lilah smiled at them over her baby's curly head. Dan's heart lurched as he recognized Travis Jardine's imprint on this little girl named Noelle. Please God, she at least would never be a slave.

Star bade the men hobble their horses where the new grass was highest. A feast was prepared, and, besides things Dan had never eaten before like young cat-tails, there were eggs, buttermilk, butter, cheese, and Sarah's honey, but no flesh of any kind.

Dan chilled, then burned, at Christy's account of Lafe's halting the women on the way to Sedalia. "No doubt he looked comical, darlin', with a diaper hanging from his hat, but, if you won't stay at the mill, at least keep to this valley."

"The farm's not worth it," Thos growled, catching his sister's hand. "Father wouldn't want you running such risks! Charlie and I . . . and Dan . . . come home, we'll rebuild the cabin and fences, if they've been burned, plow the weeds and brush out of the fields, and start over."

"This is my war, Thos." Christy touched her brother's cheek, then hurried to get Dan's fiddle out of the bark-covered long house. "Play your song, Dan," she said when she returned.

He did, but he couldn't finish it because of the hatred for Lafe Ballard that boiled up in him. His cheek burned as if the gunpowder rubbed into the cuts smoldered with invisible flame.

That night, back at the cabin, with Thos tactfully asleep in the loft, Dan held Christy, close to groaning with need and the sweetness of her mouth, her yielding body so soft to him in spite of the muscles in her arms and shoulders. When he couldn't stand it another minute, he kissed her good night and scrambled up the ladder to throw his bedroll down beside Thos.

Dan and Thos caught up with their battery at Fort Scott. The suffering of Union Indians driven from Indian Territory into Kansas had convinced President Lincoln that they should be allowed to form regiments to fight for their homeland, and the 1st Kansas was ordered to join an expedition into the territory. On the Neosho River, they picked up the 1st and 2nd Indian Regiments, which boasted 400 tall, painted Osage warriors from their southern Kansas reservation. At Baxter Springs, in the southeast corner of Kansas, they were joined by companies from the 9th, 10th, and 2nd Kansas, 2nd Ohio Cavalry, Rabb's 2nd Indiana Battery, and the 9th and 12th Regiments of Wisconsin Infantry. This Army of the Frontier, under command of Colonel William Weer, a jayhawker who had stolen plenty of fine Missouri horses in territorial days, proceeded down the Grand River.

When they had to camp some distance from this running water, Dan and the others scooped up water from slimy, stinking pools in the summer-parched creeks where Indian cattle stood to save at least their legs from buzzing, stinging swarms of green-headed flies. The water was a stew of rotting plants, manure, and sediment, but, boiled with enough coffee to turn it completely black, it had to serve.

Rebel Indians fled their breakfast campfires at Locust Grove. Dan's long-time friend who had lived with the Parkses, Tim O'Donnell, swore because the battery couldn't use its guns for fear of hitting their own troops, but Dan was relieved. What if he killed Choctaws from families that had sent money to buy the food that kept him from starving back in Ireland?

Colonel Weer stayed drunk in his tent at camp on Cabin Creek while the Indians and cavalry took Fort Gibson and, near Tahlequah, captured the Cherokee chief, John Ross, a Union sympathizer, who had signed a treaty with the Confederacy only after Federal troops had abandoned Indian Territory. Dan glimpsed the old chief pass by in a fine carriage, bound for Washington, with his pretty young Quaker wife, their daughters, the Cherokee nation's archives and treasury and wagonloads of prized belongings.

Ross's old enemy, Confederate General Stand Watie, had retreated south of the Arkansas River with his Rebel Cherokees. So had Colonel Douglas Hancock Cooper with his Choctaws, Chickasaws, and Texans. A 3rd Union Indian

Regiment was organized—swelled by Cherokees deserting from Confederate commands. The Union Indians had recovered much of their stolen livestock, and now the three Indian regiments decided to organize into a brigade to defend Indian Territory north of the Red River.

The Indian Expedition had done all that could be expected. Weer's disgusted officers placed their drunken commander under arrest. Leaving two Parrott guns with the Indian Brigade, the rest of the Army started back to Fort Scott. Half the horses were so gaunt and broken down they had to be left behind.

"These tough Western horses manage pretty well on grass, but our Ohio animals need corn and oats, poor critters," lamented Tim O'Donnell. "Some of them chewed off each other's manes and tails while they were picketed."

Dan's battery was camped with the rest of the Army of the Frontier on the banks of the Marmaton at Fort Scott when a messenger galloped into camp after supper on August 14th. "Boots and Saddles!" Tents were rolled up and stowed in wagons, cooking gear packed into mess wagons. Dan's crew harnessed the team to their gun. 2,000 infantry piled into mule-drawn wagons, cavalry mounted, Rabb's Battery rumbled up, and they were off on a forced march of four nights and three days, only halting for fifteen minutes three times daily to feed and water the mules and horses.

Confederate forces rampaging through Missouri overwhelmed Union troops at Independence on August 11th and captured twenty wagons of arms, ammunition, and supplies before marching away to join with other Rebels at a village called Lone Jack, twenty-five miles from Independence. They intended to attack Lexington. If they took and held it, they'd break Union control of the Missouri River and shipping of vital supplies to Leavenworth. It was up to this part of the Army of the Frontier, now under the personal command of General James Blunt, to drive the Rebels out of Missouri.

"Where'd all the Rebs come from?" demanded O'Donnell, on one of the brief rests.

"After they got trounced at Pea Ridge in March, there were scads of deserters," explained Harry Shepherd with the all-knowingness of a sergeant who was chief of a gun crew. "Plenty of Old Skedad Price's Missouri State Guard didn't fancy joining the regular Confederate Army to get sent East, so they've come back home. Their officers don't mind throwing in with the guerrillas who're already thick as maggots on a dead hog." He spat disgustedly. "Quantrill helped take Independence. He's got a captain's commission in the Confederate Army now, but he's still a plain old bushwhacker!"

Quantrill! The scar on Dan's face burned at the name. Where Quantrill was, Lafe Ballard wouldn't be far away. If he could kill Lafe, would the burning end?

"There's not much to stop the Rebs," Dan said, surprised that his tone was even. "Most Federal troops have been pulled out of Missouri to fight farther east, just like the real Confederate Armies."

"Didn't Missouri pass a law this year that all men between eighteen and forty-five have to join the state militia?" asked Davie Parks.

"Sure, but most of the best young men have already joined one army or the other," Dan pointed out. "Of course, lots of the militia will fight the best they can, but plenty will use being in it as an excuse to murder and steal."

Drowsing off on Raven. Falling asleep as he fed and

watered him. Eighty-four hours after leaving Fort Scott, they neared Lone Jack on the sweltering evening of August 17th to learn that the day before yesterday, less than 800 loyal Missouri militia had fought desperately, all morning, against 3,000 guerrillas and Rebel militia. What was left of the Union force had retreated to Lexington.

Thunder crashed in the northwest and heavy clouds loomed over victorious Confederates who were camped in and all around Lone Jack half a mile away. Blunt ordered his exhausted men into battle line and sent out skirmishers as the storm broke and the Confederates retreated through heavy timber.

Pursuing in the dark over a route cut up by ditches and gullies, Dan and the other artillerymen sweated in the rain, wrestled gun carriages and caissons through the mud, and battled to keep them from turning over.

Three days' and nights' chase southward, spread out for four or five miles, stopping only twice a day for an hour to rest and feed themselves and hard-pushed animals that had never had a chance to recover from the Indian Expedition.

"If you and I are still alive when this war's over," Dan said to Raven as he slipped on the nosebag, "I'll buy or steal you, boy, and the rest of your life you'll get corn, oats, and fine grass right up to your belly!"

Blunt's advance cavalry caught up with the Rebels several times and skirmished, but the Rebels slipped away. At Carthage, loyal Missouri cavalry took over the pursuit and drove the Confederates into the southeast corner of Missouri while Blunt's command toiled back to Fort Scott.

They weren't there long. Late in August, General Thomas Hindman was put in command of the Confederate District of Arkansas, which included Missouri and Indian Territory. By sending armed squads around a countryside from which all able-bodied men had supposedly been sent east to fight, he forced 20,000 unwilling Arkansans into his army—and quite a few into the 1st Arkansas Union Cavalry that was beginning to organize. The Confederacy had passed a law conscripting for three years all able-bodied men between eighteen and thirty-five who owned less than twenty slaves. Naturally those who had no slaves felt they shouldn't have to fight in the place of those who did.

Rebel victories at Independence and Lone Jack fired General Hindman with hope that he could win Missouri. He sent, northward, three regiments of Missouri militia under Colonel Jo Shelby, Stand Watie's Cherokees, and General Cooper's brigade of Chickasaws and Choctaws. Cooper had only been a colonel when chased south of the Arkansas River about seven weeks earlier, but now he had taken the flamboyant and poetic General Pike's place as Indian Commissioner and commander of the Confederate Indians.

Dan's battery, with units of the 1st and 2nd Brigades of Blunt's Army, rolled up after these Rebels had fought with Union soldiers all around the stone fences of a farm outside the little college town of Newtonia, south of Carthage.

Hogs were coming to investigate soldiers of the 9th Wisconsin who lay dead in a little field, stripped of their arms and clothing. Dan joined in the hasty building of enough rail pens to keep the bodies safe from the hogs till they could be buried. Several of the Wisconsin boys looked younger than Davie Parks, whose face was pale and clammy as he helped Dan hoist life-emptied bodies and drop them inside the rails.

Fighting from plum thickets and rail fences, the Union men forced the Rebels to take cover in the town. All that afternoon, the guns loaded and fired. Dan had emptied his canteen hours ago. His arm and shoulder ached from yanking the lanyard, but the cannonading held the enemy at bay till twilight when the order came to withdraw.

Rebel cavalry poured out of the town, shouting their glee, but fresh Union troops came up to stiffen the weary ones and masked a battery behind clumps of post and black-jack oak. Trained on the Confederates spurring after the foe, the guns hurled grape and canister that blasted men and horses into heaps where some struggled and others were deathly still.

The cavalry fled. Union soldiers hurried to Shoal Creek where they could water their animals, splash their own dusty faces, and drink their fill. That was on September 30th. On October 2nd, Blunt marched up with the rest of his army and prepared to take Newtonia.

The Confederates abandoned the town without a fight and made for the Arkansas border. Dan winced at seeing where cannon balls had torn through college buildings and houses, but it wasn't only the *buzz* of flies and stench that sickened him when he saw the ripped and mangled horses, especially an artillery team—all six animals —slaughtered by an exploding shell.

Supplies were short and the hard-used mules and horses needed grain. The Army of the Frontier foraged what the retreating Rebels had left behind. Union farmers were sup-posed to be given chits of payment, but it made Dan ache to see women, whose men were off fighting on one side or the other, come into camp to plead with an officer for that last side of bacon, the last load of corn or wheat, the pet milk cow so needed by the scrawny children, the horse needed to plow and carry grain to the mill.

More than once, Dan, Davie, Thos, and Tim O'Donnell—for he'd known hunger, too—gave women and children most of their rations of hardtack, bacon, coffee, and sugar, keeping just enough to sustain them along with windfall apples, papaws, and wild grapes.

Shelby and his Missourians took shelter in the Boston Mountains near Fayetteville, but scouts reported that Cooper and Watie had collected between 4,000 and 7,000 Indian troops at long abandoned Fort Wayne, just over the Arkansas line in the Cherokee Nation.

After an all night march, Blunt struck on the morning of October 22nd with a flying squadron of cavalry and howitzers while the rest of his army followed, including Dan's battery. They arrived hours after the whole Rebel battery was captured and Cooper's force raced for the Arkansas River covered by Stand Watie's more disciplined men.

To keep Confederates out of Missouri, Union encampments were scattered for 100 miles along the Wire Road as far as Wilson's Creek, some at Pea Ridge battlefield. Blunt's men were camped southwest of Bentonville, at the southern end of this Union line late in November, when scouts dashed in with word that General John Marmaduke, a soft-spoken West Pointer whose father had been governor of Missouri, was advancing with artillery and 7,000 cavalry— Jo Shelby's Iron Brigade, Missouri militia, assorted bushwhackers, and Quantrill's men.

Would Lafe be with them? Dan rubbed his scar to ease the stinging. Quantrill had gone to Richmond to try to get a higher commission than captain. The South had to be desperate to commission a bushwhacker, but Quantrill could scarcely be worse than Doc Jennison or Jim Lane who had Union commissions.

General Hindman would join Marmaduke with 25,000 men. It was clear that he hoped to win back northwest Arkansas and Indian Territory, and, from that strength, invade Missouri.

At the hamlet of Cane Hill, Blunt struck Marmaduke full

blast on the morning of November 28th with 5,000 cavalry, howitzers, and light artillery. Dan's battery of heavy Parrotts, positioned with the infantry, caught up after the battle had turned into a race. All Dan's crew could do was send a few shells after Rebels who were a mile away, scrambling into the rocky foothills of the Boston Mountains.

To prepare for Hindman, Blunt telegraphed for reinforcements, and had all the wheat to be found in the area taken to mills and ground to feed his men. His supplies had to come from Leavenworth 250 miles away, so the more his army could live off the country, the better for them—and the worse for the farmers in that fertile region renowned for its peach and apple brandy, its grain, potatoes, and fruit.

General Francis Herron, commander of the cantonment at Wilson's Creek, got telegraphed orders to aid Blunt and was on the march in a few hours' time with 6,000 men, their knapsacks carried in wagons to speed them. While Hindman came half that distance, they had to cover 125 miles, chewing raw pork and hardtack as they marched thirty-five miles each twenty-four hours, snatching an hour of sleep whenever they could.

On December 7th, this exhausted, footsore Army encountered Hindman's two-mile-long battle line near Prairie Grove church among farms with rail-fenced fields of withered cornstalks and bare orchards. The *boom* of cannon reached Blunt at Cane Hill, eight miles south.

Bugles sounded, drums rolled, and up the Fayetteville road galloped Blunt, cavalry at his heels, batteries and infantry following as fast as they could. This was the first time the 1st Kansas Battery had really been under fire. Ordered to the right to meet the charge of General Daniel Marsh Frost's entire division, they were raked with rifle fire before they were in position.

Dan crouched low on Raven's outstretched neck. The coarse black mane whipped his face. His lips stung with the salt taste of the wheel horse's sweat. Raven's flared nostrils showed crimson. His eyes were wild. The postilions ahead and all around lashed their horses at each heart-bursting leap. Raven gave all he could without a whip, but at the gunner's shout—"Faster! Faster!"—Dan echoed the cry in Raven's pricked-back ear. Dan's gunner was red-headed Tim O'Donnell and their chief-of-piece was O'Donnell's brother-in-law, big, black-haired Sergeant Harry Shepherd.

Madly spinning wheels of gun carriages and caissons hurtled and clanged from rock to rock through the trees while artillerymen hung on for dear life. Cavalry, bent over saddle horns, spilled out of the woods fringing this Arkansas prairie of withered cornstalks and December-naked orchards. The horsemen spurred past guns and infantry, who, mostly hatless and coatless, held tightly to muskets and ammunition.

The Rebels occupied a wooded ridge to the south. Stocky, black-mustached General Blunt, all alone on the field at first, waved guns and troops into position. Dan almost fell off Raven and helped unlimber the ten-pound Parrott.

Here came the Rebs, trying to overrun Blunt before he formed his battle lines, but men were grouping by regimental banners with the Stars and Stripes floating above them all.

"Load with canister!"

Davie Parks brought the round from the limber chest in his leather haversack, and put the tin can filled with eighty-five, one-ounce lead balls in the muzzle. Mac Ford, a skinny, freckled Missourian, rammed it home, and Bob Hendricks, dark eyes blazing, trained the gun according to O'Donnell's orders.

"Ready!" Hendricks pricked the powder bag through the vent near the bottom of the barrel; Dan hooked the lanyard to the primer, stuck it in the vent, and moved to the side and back while Hendricks covered the vent with his mittened hand to prevent an accidental discharge.

"Fire!" Dan pulled the lanyard. The charge exploded, belching the canister with its scattering balls into the Rebels who were firing muskets as they charged.

After two rounds, a thick cloud of the white smoke made from the black powder created a shroud. Through it, Dan glimpsed an officer urging on his men, saw him and those around him fall as if scythed down.

Over and over. "Load!" "Ready!" "Fire!"

And then O'Donnell looked at Dan through the smoke just as a cannon ball carried off his head.

Somehow, they went on. Harry Shepherd yelled at them to load as he took his brother-in-law's place as gunner. After a final twilight artillery duel closed the day, setting straw stacks on fire, the crew buried O'Donnell in his corporal's uniform under a black-jack oak overlooking the creek. Shepherd cut off a lock of curly red hair to send to O'Donnell's sister, Peggy, along with O'Donnell's few personal belongings, before placing the battered forage cap over O'Donnell's face. Tears wet the rocks they heaped on the mound to keep out digging animals. Tim O'Donnell, friend of Dan's childhood, who, like Andy McHugh, had crossed the ocean and half America to die. Dan clung to the grace that at least his friend had lived a number of good years in Ohio, rather than having starved as a lad in some County Clare ditch.

The supply wagons had not caught up and they'd had nothing to eat all day. They filled their bellies with water from the creek. Dan and Thos put Davie between them as they burrowed into a straw stack to escape the cold.

Next morning, they expected the battle to resume, but Hindman had sent a flag of truce, asking for twelve hours to take his dead and wounded off the field. Blunt agreed although most of the Union wounded had already been taken to a field hospital behind the lines.

Stretcher-bearers and burial details went out from both armies. Ladies came in wagons and carriages to help collect the wounded and take them to Fayetteville. Dan and Davie helped bury the dead. Some of Herron's men, who had not a wound, had died in the chilly night, exhausted from their grueling march and the battle.

"Our guns must have got these," Dan said as he and Davie approached bodies that lay close together as reaped grain. He bent to pick up a bullet. "This hasn't been fired."

"Here's more like it," said Davie.

Dan stared at the stiffened bodies in the bloody muck as an infantryman began to scoop bullets up in handfuls. "They bit the bullets off and spat them out. They only fired blank loads." Dan spoke through a lump in his throat. "These'll be Union men Hindman forced into his army . . . men who wouldn't fire on their country's flag."

Davie's eyes widened. "Look over there! The straw stacks that caught fire last night!"

The breeze carried the unmistakable smell of burned flesh from the black remnants of the stacks. Hogs rooted through the ashes, emerged with a leg, an arm, a head, intestines, and fought over these prizes. Wounded and dying soldiers had crawled into the straw for shelter and died in the blaze.

"Look what this lad had in his pocket!" The freckled doughboy picking up bullets flourished a leaflet. "Did you ever hear such a mess of lies?"

Dan read the beginning. "Sounds like good advice, especially to fresh recruits. 'Single out your target, aim as low as the knees, shoot officers when possible, kill artillery horses. . . .' "

"You ain't read far enough!"

Remember that the enemy you engage has no feelings of mercy or kindness toward you. His ranks are made up of Pin Indians, free Negroes, Southern Tories, Kansas jayhawkers, and hired Dutch cut-throats. These bloody ruffians have invaded your country, stolen and destroyed your property, murdered your neighbors, outraged your women, driven your children from their homes, and defiled the graves of your kindred. . . .

"Reckon it's all in your point of view." Dan squinted toward the nearest living Confederates. "Say, they're picking up weapons and ammunition, instead of their dead and wounded!"

Just then one of Blunt's staff rode up. In tones loud enough to reach Dan, he told the Confederates to carry out their proper duty. The message was delivered around the field; most of the Rebels departed, leaving many of their dead to be buried by the enemy, and their wounded to be sent as prisoners to Fayetteville's churches and college buildings that had been turned into hospitals.

A new buzz spread through the Union burial teams. "Hindman sneaked off in the night . . . muffled his wheels with blankets! That flag of truce was a trick to give him a whole day more to get ahead of us . . . and scavenge weapons!"

About then the supply wagons clattered up, rations were shared out, and Dan's crew feasted on water-soaked hardtack fried with bacon, and strong coffee.

Hindman didn't give up easily. Toward the end of December, Blunt's Army was resting near Cane Hill when word came that at Van Buren, on the Arkansas River, Hindman had new supplies and was organizing for yet another campaign.

What a time the batteries had getting their guns and caissons over the mountains! It took double teams and the crews and other soldiers hauling with ropes and pushing the wheels up rocky ledges, but, after twenty hours, Blunt's and Herron's commands struggled out of the mountains.

Encountering the 1st Texas Cavalry, Herron's cavalry chased them through Van Buren and shelled the steam ferry they tried to escape on with howitzers. Hindman's battery opened up from across the river, bombarding the town, but the light cannon were no match for Blunt's two long-range Parrotts.

Cavalry and howitzers forced four supply-laden Confederate steamships to surrender. Great was the joy among the Union troops to have all the molasses they wanted and plenty of sugar! The *Rose Douglas* alone yielded 4,300 bushels of corn, so the weary horses had their feast, too. Also, the next day, the steamships could carry the Union men and horses across the river to the Confederate camps.

Once again, Hindman's Army retreated in the night. He abandoned Fort Smith, destroying two steamboats and all the supplies he couldn't take with him. Blunt, having driven the Confederates well south of the Arkansas River, burned the ferry and four captured steamboats along with 15,000 bushels of corn and other supplies he couldn't transport.

Once back north of the Boston Mountains, there was a chase after Marmaduke, Jo Shelby, and Quantrill's men who tried to capture Springfield. Fought off by the garrison, they pillaged back into Arkansas and left a song in their wake: "Jo Shelby's at your stable door. Where's your mule, oh, where's your mule?"

Union men shouted it out as they marched along, along with the three most favorite of all—"John Brown's Body", the stirring new "Battle Hymn of the Republic", and their own version of "Dixie".

Away down South in the land of traitors,
Rebel hearts and Union haters,
Look away, look away, look away
to the traitor's land.

From Springfield, knee deep in February snow, the 1st Kansas Battery moved to Fort Scott, then to Lawrence in April. Dan had to chuckle bitterly as he remembered how a party of important citizens met the battery four miles out of town and suggested they camp on the Wakarusa rather than in Lawrence whose citizens didn't want their peace and quiet disturbed by rowdy soldiers. That didn't matter much to Dan. Didn't he have two weeks' leave? He'd soon be with Christy.

As he roused that morning, he draped Christy's blanket to air over a budding oak limb. He'd taken the best care of it he could, but it was frayed in places. Dan craved strong coffee, but the preserve can in which he cooked it had burned through yesterday and he hadn't taken time to re-place it. He wanted to spend every minute that he could with Christy. Thos and Davie had diarrhea and had urged him not to wait for them. He put on his coat with its corporal's stripes—he was a gunner now, replacing poor Tim O'Donnell—tugged on his boots, gave Raven a nosebag of corn, and chewed hardtack dunked in water from the Marais des Cygnes while rolling his blanket. He couldn't wrap it in the oilcloth because that protected the calico he'd bought at Fort Scott. He'd spent all his pay at the sutler's for the cloth and a knapsack full of treats.

He'd thought about wearing his artilleryman's sword to impress Christy, but decided that was more trouble than it was worth, which was about the value of the weapon in battle. As Raven jogged east of Osawatomie across the prairie broken by those peculiar mounds, Dan wondered why Andy McHugh and Tim O'Donnell still called to him from dreams when he'd seen so many men die since Wilson's Creek and Prairie Grove. That battle had killed Tim, but surely crushed all hopes of the Confederacy to possess Missouri.

It was noon when Dan stopped at the Parkses' mill to say that Davie and Thos were plagued with the trots but would be along when they could stay on a horse longer than they were off it. He was embraced, questioned, and fed, but not till Susie assured him that Christy had just, day before yesterday, brought letters to be posted to him and Thos. Relieved, Dan produced his gifts of canned pineapple, salmon, peas from France, and taffy for the children that Susie put up till after the meal.

"Where's Lydia?" Dan asked, when she didn't appear for dinner.

Uncle Simeon shook his white head. "When she heard that Missus Ware had gone to be a nurse, nothing would do her but to go. You were at Prairie Grove. So was Lydia, after the battle . . . Missus Ware, too. They came with a wagon for the wounded. What a waste . . . what a terrible waste of our best young men! Truly we are grinding up our seed corn."

Remembering Tim, Dan swallowed hard. "Yes, between twelve and thirteen hundred were lost on either side." How cold numbers were! Each of those men was mourned by family and friends, would be achingly missed all the days of their lives just as Susie and old Catriona mourned Andy. And his little son would never, ever know him.

Blue-eyed Letty Parks confided that she had just turned eight, and had charge of her sturdy dark-haired brother Danny, and her cousin Andy, red-headed, thin, and quick. The boys, two-and-a-half years old, nodded yes, they would like a ride on Raven when Dan offered.

Owen walked with Dan as he led the horse around. "I feel like a slacker." Owen's brown eyes were troubled. "Here I am, safe at home, while my kid brother and you and Thos Ware dodge cannon balls."

"You were at Wilson's Creek. No one who was needs to apologize for getting out when his enlistment was up."

"I know. Close to a quarter of all the soldiers were lost. To top that, you've got to look back to the charge of the Light Brigade where over a third died. But I still feel like Davie's taking my place."

"Owen, you have two small children and Susie McHugh's boy to raise, not to mention Catriona and your mother-in-law to provide for. Uncle Simeon needs you or Davie . . . and Davie was busting to go."

"But. . . ."

"With guerrillas swarming over the western half of Missouri, there's no telling when they'll raid across the border. There'll be precious few regular troops to stop them." Dan looked ruefully at his foster-brother. "*I* feel guilty for racketing off and leaving Christy alone."

"Scarcely alone. Not with Sarah Morrow and those women in the valley. We've begged her to come here, Dan, but she won't." Owen reached up his arms to scoop all three children off Raven. "Uncle Dan has to go, youngsters. Give him a hug and thank him."

Letty not only hugged him, she touched his scar and

kissed it. The deadened tissue couldn't feel the moth-like brush of her lips, but a painful tingling shot through Dan like that caused by stirring a leg or arm that has gone to sleep. He couldn't repulse her sweetness, yet he wished, as if it might contaminate her, that she hadn't kissed Lafe Ballard's mark. It couldn't quench the brimstone smoldering there. Only Lafe's blood could do that.

It was twilight when he came in sight of the happy house. A curl of smoke rose from the chimney. *Intruders? Or might it be Christy?* One part of his mind hoped it was, while the saner part knew it was risky for her to be there. He didn't want to scare her, nor did he wish to give some bushwhacker a chance to shoot him down. He compromised by reining Raven in near the cover of some trees.

"Hello! Anybody home?"

Christy ran out and toward him.

He came out of the saddle to meet her. "You . . . you shouldn't have rushed out here like this!" he chided, when at last he made himself draw back. "What if it hadn't been me?"

Her eyes sparkled even in the dim light. "Do you think I don't know your voice?" she scoffed. "Let's turn Raven into the pasture and have supper. Sarah and I are staying here while we plow weeds out of the corn." Her voice rose. "Where's Thos?"

"He'll be along," Dan assured her. "Has a little stomach complaint, is all."

Lad and Lass came over to greet Raven. Dan put his saddle over the edge of a manger in the barn, and dropped his knapsack to give Sarah a hearty embrace as she hurried out to greet him. War stripped away conventions and Dan was mightily grateful that she was Christy's friend.

"How long can you stay?" Christy asked as they walked to the house.

"Ten days here. Took me two to come, and I'll need that to get back."

There was no bread, but the stew was thick and good. Dan had two bowls while briefly relating where the battery had traveled these past ten months. He didn't tell them about Tim O'Donnell.

The spring night brought a chill. Sarah built up a fire and brewed sassafras tea. He didn't want to talk about where he'd been and what he'd done since he saw them last. Christy already knew that her mother and Lydia Parks had gone to the battlefield at Prairie Grove and carried away the wounded, but Dan had to admit he hadn't seen them.

He briefly sketched the battery's travels and told them all the funny tales he could, including the many ways to vary hardtack. They told him that baby Noelle was taking her first teetering steps, Beth had almost complete charge of Richie and was teaching him to read and write, and that corn promised well, both in the valley and here in the field Jonathan had broken from wilderness.

"Tomorrow we'll go to the valley so you can see Beth and the others and bring back your fiddle," Christy said.

Sarah yawned and stretched. "I'm pretty tired, folks. Good night and happy dreams." She disappeared into the bedroom part of the double cabin.

Into a deep, pulsing silence, when Dan could scarcely breathe, Christy stretched out her hand and rested it on his. "Danny. . . ."

He turned her hand over and kissed the calloused palm. "I'm mighty tired, too, sweetheart. Got some quilts I can spread in the loft or shall I get the blanket you made me?"

After a moment, her jaw set. "There's an extra cornshuck mattress and a quilt . . . even a pillow. I'll make up a bed for you."

"No need you climbing up there. Just give me the things."

He was surprised that she didn't argue further. In a few minutes she was back, heaped with bedding. Lordy, how could he stand ten days—and nights—of this when she didn't understand, couldn't help him? He'd have to take himself off to the woods at night or stay in the valley.

He spread the rustling mattress by the lamp light from below and folded a quilt so it was both beneath and over him. The pillow smelled of Christy. He started to toss it down to her, but stopped. He couldn't have her, but he could have the comfort of something she had used. He undressed as the lamp below was extinguished, and, although he'd thought he couldn't get to sleep easily, he huddled into Christy's pillow and seemed to fall into sleep.

He dreamed of her, as he often had, but this was so real. She was in his arms, bending over him so that her hair veiled his face, and then she brought him into her. There was a gasp as his hardness met resistance. Then that was gone and there was only softness, moist satin that yielded and clung at the same time. He groaned with release and woke.

Slowly, as she stroked his back and shoulders, he realized it was not a dream. Horrified, he tried to pull away, but she held him. "We have ten nights, Danny."

After a moment, he drew her close. "All right. But tomorrow we'll go to the mill and get Uncle Simeon to marry us." He sighed and buried his head on her breast. "Oh, Christy, I tried. . . ."

"Well, now you just need to stay alive and come back," she whispered.

He yearned to take her again, awake and knowing everything, but he was sure she was tender, and so he held her and they slept.

Sarah plowed weeds from the rows of young corn next morning while Dan and Christy went to the valley and invited the women to their wedding. Hildy couldn't take the chance of being caught by guerrillas and Star said she would rather not leave the valley, but Lilah and Hester came, along with Beth and Richie.

If the Parkses were startled to see Dan again so quickly, and with such a mission, they didn't betray it. Letty and Beth chattered while looking after small Danny, Andy, and Richie. Susie made a bouquet of daffodils and lent her ring to Christy. It was a bright day, so they gathered outside under the fresh-leafed trees. Christy wore her least faded dress and Dan had brushed his uniform.

Simeon read from the Song of Solomon. *Set me as a seal upon thine heart, as a seal upon thine arm: for love is strong as death. . . . Many waters cannot quench love; neither can the floods drown it.*

They pledged each other in the Quaker manner, kissed sweetly, and then were surrounded and embraced by happily weeping friends, including old Catriona McHugh. Even Owen had to blink as he shook Dan's hand and clasped his shoulder.

Susie insisted they have dinner. She had baked that morning, and there was a pound cake as well as fresh bread and butter to enjoy with a chowder of onions, potatoes, peas, and dried corn. Catriona set out jars of pickles and preserves, and there was real coffee as well as buttermilk.

As they traveled home, Dan, with Christy holding onto

his waist, saw that Lilah, mounted on Lad with Noelle in front of her, was shaken with smothered sobs. Hester, who rode with Sarah on Lass, nudged the mare close and put her arm around the young woman. "You've got beautiful little Noelle, dear. After the war. . . ."

"After the war, I'll still look black to Master Travis."

"He won't be your master," Dan cut in. "And who knows? It'll be a whole new world, Lilah."

She straightened and managed a wobbly smile. "Bad of me to cry on your wedding day. I . . . I do for sure and always wish you happy."

Sarah said bracingly: "Listen, my girl, if that Travis doesn't know how lucky he is, there'll be plenty of other men."

Lilah didn't answer.

At the Ware cabin, Sarah grinned. "You honeymooners can have the place to yourselves. I'll go on with Lilah and Hester, but, mind, I'll be back in the morning to plow those weeds!"

"I'll plow, too," Dan promised. "I want to do all I can while I'm here."

"Oh, you will," laughed Sarah, and left them, blushing, suddenly shy, although that didn't last for long.

CHAPTER EIGHT

It was late August, four months since Dan had ridden away. The corn, so young and green then, was now stripped of blades fodder and today Christy would start cutting the plump, hardening corn ears off the bare stalks. Sarah had taken Lass, laden with fodder, to the valley so late that she'd spent the night, but she'd be back by noon.

It seemed strange that Hildy was no longer in the valley, but last month Justus had sent word to the Parkses that should his wife come to them, they could tell her that he, being a good blacksmith, had been put on more or less permanent duty at Leavenworth and had quarters next to the smithy. If Hildy could come to him, he'd send money for the journey. Simeon and Susie had taken her to Leavenworth in their wagon, Hildy posing as Susie's maid the few times they were questioned. Hildy had wept to leave Richie but knew he'd be fine with the other women and Beth to care for him.

Smiling to think of that reunion, Christy yearned for the next time she'd be with Dan—and prayed that time would come. At least her morning sickness was over. Christy finished her mush and sassafras tea. When clothed, she didn't show, but, when she undressed, she could see just the slightest rounding. Four months now. The baby should come near the middle of January. She hadn't written this news to her mother in the hospital in Louisville, Kentucky. Much as Christy wanted to have her mother with her during the birth, sick and wounded soldiers needed her more.

Maybe the war would be over by then. Christy drew in a long breath and closed her eyes. *Oh Dan! Danny!* If he could be with her, too—but she didn't dare hope for that. The war showed no sign of ending quickly, even though on July 4th Grant had taken Vicksburg.

This gives the Union control of the Mississippi and cuts the South in half, Dan had written jubilantly. *No supplies or troops from Texas and Louisiana can get through, which hits the Rebels hard. We were camped at Rolla when the news of Vicksburg came. Our battery officers bought six kegs of beer and set them on cracker boxes scattered around camp. You can bet we celebrated!*

On July 3rd, the Union won the hard-fought three-day battle of Gettysburg in Pennsylvania. Instead of pursuing General Lee, five regiments with Gatling guns, a terrible new invention, were ordered from Gettysburg to New York City to quell an ugly draft riot in New York, four days of terror in which 1,000 people were killed.

Dan's next letter told about the battery getting off the train at St. Louis. *We felt like we'd been dropped in the middle of another world. Close to 200,000 people live here and it looked like all of them were in the streets that were lit up almost plain as day. We didn't like it much when the lieutenant told us we had to pull over to let civilian wagons pass, but we finally got to an old stockyard where we were supposed to camp. I wasn't about to spread your blanket in that mess, so I climbed over a board fence and landed in the nicest thick grass you can imagine. Got the finest rest I've ever had in the Army and woke up at "Reveille" to stare up at a marble tombstone! I'd spent the night in the Wesleyan cemetery!*

The battery was sent by train to Cincinnati, in case General John Morgan besieged the city on his dare-devil raid through Indiana and Ohio. *We saw neither hide nor whisker of him. His little band was being chased by 50,000 men. When he was finally surrounded and had to give up, he had only 336 left of his 2,400 cavalry he'd brought from Kentucky.*

Dan was back in St. Louis now, at Camp Jackson. Thos and I did as you asked, sweetheart, and visited Charlie's wife at her sister's mansion. The colored maid didn't want to let us in, but Melissa heard us and welcomed us graciously. I can't say the same for her sister, whose husband is in a Union prison. Joel is a handsome, sturdy, happy, little lad with a strong look of Charlie. Melissa can't write to Charlie, but once in a great while he gets a letter to her by using tobacco to bribe a Union picket to send it. He and Travis are with Price's command at Little Rock.

It was good to hear Joely was thriving, and have some news of Charlie. Melissa seldom wrote. Trying not to be hurt by that, Christy told herself that Melissa couldn't be blamed for avoiding reminders of that terrible winter when she'd lost her parents and Rose Haven and had to shelter in a cave.

Resting her hand over the baby, Christy wished it would quicken so that she could be sure he was really there, almost halfway through the time before she could hold him in her arms. *Him?* She laughed softly at herself.

Of course she wanted a son, with Dan's flaming hair and smoke-gray eyes, but when he'd responded to her news with proud excitement, he'd hoped for a daughter. *Could we call her Bridget Ellen or Ellen Bridget for my sister and your mother?*

Boy or girl, she prayed the baby wouldn't be two or three years old before it got to know its father, but she vowed to be eternally grateful if Dan came home at all.

Tying on her sunbonnet, she got a corn knife from the barn—Dan said that bayonets would make splendid corn knives after the war—and trundled the wheelbarrow to the field. It was a laborious way of moving the corn to the crib, but she didn't risk the horses, even Lass with her feigned crippling, more than absolutely necessary.

Christy knelt beside her father's stone. In December, it would be two years since he had been shot in the act of welcoming the guerrillas. She hoped he knew she was holding the farm, but hoped he didn't know how bad things were along the border.

Most Union troops had been ordered east of the Mississippi to fight battles where, as at Gettysburg, the North lost 20,000 men. General Thomas Ewing, commander of the recently created District of the Border, had less than 3,000 men to garrison and protect eastern Kansas, western Missouri, and guard the supply line from Leavenworth to Fort Scott and General Blunt's District of the Frontier. In May, guerrillas had attacked Diamond Springs on the Santa Fé Trail, 100 miles into Kansas on the western fringe of settlement. They held up a stage, robbed, killed, and slipped back into Missouri with considerable plunder. At the same time, on the Osage reservation in southern Kansas, sixteen Confederates, carrying orders to recruit Southern sympathizers in Colorado and New Mexico, were killed by the Osages. A month later, guerrillas dashed over the border to raid Shawnee. No small Union force in Missouri was safe from ambush.

Lacking enough troops to hunt down the guerrillas who scattered to their homes or the woods after a foray, Ewing set up stations along the border about twelve miles apart, one at Trading Post. The distances between were patrolled every hour. Invading guerrillas were to be instantly pursued, help sent for if the band outnumbered the soldiers, and threatened settlements warned.

Meanwhile, George Hoyt's Red Legs terrorized Missouri, burning homes, stealing horses and mules, and killing men in front of their families. Hoyt, the Massachusetts lawyer who had headed John Brown's defense, had become captain of John Brown, Jr.'s Company K of the 7th Kansas when ill health forced Brown to resign in May of 1862, about the time Jennison resigned command of the regiment. After the 7th was ordered east, partly to stop its jayhawking in Missouri, Hoyt convinced his superiors that the climate of Mississippi had him at death's door. He resigned his commission in the summer of 1862, and came back to Kansas to lead the Red Legs, so called from their red leather leggings. Jennison, now recruiting for the 15th Kansas Volunteer Cavalry to be used only in protecting Kansas, was suspected of being in cahoots with the Red Legs.

This border war was waged by devils on both sides. Yet as Christy cut off the ears of corn, her spirit calmed to see the cardinal bring seeds to his fourth brood of the summer and glimpse the yellow-billed cuckoo or rain crow nesting for the first time.

As the day warmed, she unbuttoned the top of her dress. Before long she'd put inserts in the sides to accommodate her swelling breasts. It was good luck Danny—or Bridget Ellen!—would be able to inherit Noelle's outgrown things, since there was no wool. Next spring, if the war dragged on, Christy had better plant cotton or flax, if she could get some seed. Even Sarah was getting ragged, for she'd shared the dresses made from the gay materials lavished on her by Lige, her husband.

One of the hounds rose, lifted his nose to catch the breeze, and bayed. In an instant, all the pack was up. Above the pounding blood in her ears, Christy heard the *jingle* of spurs and bits, the *thud* of hoofs, the *creak* of saddles.

Could she hide? Get to the cavern across the creek? She

caught up her skirts to run. A volley of shots froze her. All but two hounds fell, most of them yelping and writhing. Calling the dogs that lived, she ran toward them and hauled them close against her while keeping her grip on the knife.

The wounded dogs tried to crawl to her. She dragged the two unhurt blue ticks to where she could shield them, along with three others, and straightened to face the oncoming horsemen, a score of them.

Fine mounts, brightly embroidered shirts, braces of pistols, and plumed hats proclaimed them guerrillas. Some led pack animals loaded with plunder and most led a horse or mule. If Bill Anderson was in command—but he wouldn't have let them shoot the hounds. A redbone that had crept under her skirts whimpered, twitched, and went still.

The man in the lead swept off his hat, flourishing the black plume. The sun turned his fair hair to spun silver. "Step away from those curs," Lafe Ballard said in a pleasant voice. "I don't like to be barked at."

Christy spread her skirts around as many animals as she could. Lafe raised an eyebrow, shrugged, and said to his men: "Finish the dogs you can hit without hurting my old schoolmate."

The men used the hounds for targets, riddling them.

"Not as much fun as killing the damned Lawrence Abolitionists," laughed a bulky young man Christy dazedly recognized as Tom Maddux.

"Lawrence?" Christy echoed.

Lafe smiled. "We hit that nest of Red Legs and nigger-loving psalm singers at dawn three days ago. Oh, not just my boys, Christy. Colonel Quantrill had four hundred and fifty men."

Tom Maddux chuckled. "Burned the town. Killed every man we found, 'cept some old friends of Colonel Quantrill.

A hundred and fifty or more! You should have seen 'em crawl and beg for their lives!" He added virtuously: "We never killed a single woman, but I was hard put to it several times to reach around one who was hanging onto her man, so I could blast him."

"We roasted some of 'em, too," added a barrel-chested redhead. He spat at a dead hound. "Ole Jim Lane got away, though . . . damn his eyes."

Even in her horror, Christy wondered how many of the slaughtered men had been in the delegation that had visited Dan's battery only four months ago and asked them to camp beyond the town that didn't want soldiers roistering through the streets.

"Too bad some of them nigger recruits got away across the river," Maddux said, sighing. "They need a lesson, what with that Harriet Tubman leadin' nigger troops into South Carolina, burnin' plantations, and freein' slaves. They do say she brought out eight hunnerd of 'em."

"Don't forget them Massachusetts nigs that attacked Fort Wagner close to Charleston," put in the redhead, who spat again. "Hell, some black sergeant's up for the Medal of Honor. Makes me want to puke!"

"Honey Springs down in Indian Territory last month was worse," growled a man with a bushy black beard. "Blunt's niggers and Union Injuns whupped the tar out of twice as many of Cooper's Texans and Southern Injuns!"

"Cooper claimed his powder was wet," said Maddux. "Stand Watie wasn't there to lead the Cherokees, and, anyhow, Blunt had white troops, too . . . even some of that bunch from Colorado."

The redhead spat a third time. "Hey, when has Cooper ever won anything like an even fight? He had three or four hundred pairs of handcuffs. He reckoned them niggers would jest walk into 'em, so's he could give 'em back to their masters! Well, the niggers and Pin Injuns sashayed north with the handcuffs . . . and Cooper's supplies!"

Maddux wrinkled his brow, then thought of something cheerful. "At least up at Lawrence we killed some of the niggers Jim Lane stole out of Missouri. Maybe it'll be a lesson to 'em."

Lafe listened to his men with one leg cocked across the saddle horn. Now he grinned at Christy as if reading her one forlorn hope. "You'd better not count on any favors from Bill Anderson, my dear. You probably know Ewing's been exiling or imprisoning the womenfolk of guerrillas. Three of Bill's sisters and some other females were jailed on the second floor of an old brick building in Kansas City. It caved in August Thirteenth. Damn' Yanks may've tunneled under it on purpose. Killed five of the girls."

"Not . . . not Josie?" choked Christy.

"Yes. Josephine Anderson, all of fourteen years old, died in the wreckage. Her sister Mary is likely crippled for life."

Maddux's eyes bulged. "Did you see that silk cord Bill carries? He started tying knots in it when he heard about his sisters." Maddux giggled. "Bill tied a bunch of knots before we rode out of Lawrence."

Sparring for time, although she didn't want Sarah to walk into this, Christy asked: "How did you get through Ewing's border patrols?"

"Colonel Quantrill's scouts watched," said Lafe. "When the patrol passed, we knew there wouldn't be another one along for an hour. That was long enough to get across."

"You must have all the troops in central Kansas after you!"

"They were on our trail in a hurry, but we broke up after we crossed the border above Westport." Even in her terror,

Christy gave thanks they hadn't struck Trading Post or the mill. "We know the country and Ewing's men don't," Lafe boasted. "They'll never catch us." Lafe turned to his men. "Ride along with Maddux to his folks' place. His ma'll be glad to cook up some of the fancy vittles you got in Lawrence." His smile chilled Christy to the bone. "I'll have dinner with my old neighbor. Catch up with you at Madduxes tonight."

Would she be dead by then? Or just wish she were?

Lafe waved an expansive hand. "Take all the corn you can carry for your horses, boys. We won't find many fields between here and Arkansas."

Plowing, planting, weeding—all the months of care, the main winter food for herself and her friends. "Tom . . . ," Christy began. She broke off as she sensed Lafe's pleasure. He wanted her to beg. Trying not to show that she felt a pang at the sound of each breaking stalk, Christy said: "Let me take care of the dogs, Lafe. Then I'll fix your dinner."

He leveled a revolver at one of the bristling hounds. Christy knelt, embracing the animals so that he could scarcely kill them without hitting her. After a moment he lowered the gun, but rested it on the saddle horn.

"I expect you'll be more . . . hospitable, if you don't want me to kill the brutes. Throw the knife here on the ground and see to them quickly then."

Of the three wounded dogs sheltered by her skirts, an old blue tick, Sam, bleeding profusely from several bullets, licked her hand, feebly moved his tail, and put his head against her foot as if very, very tired. By the time Christy could see through her tears, Sam's eyes were starting to glaze.

Chita, a young redbone, heavy with her first litter, was grazed along one flank. Sarah's favorite hound, Blue Boy, had a shattered right forepaw. It might have to be cut off, but, for now, Christy decided to put on Hester's salve and a bandage.

Lafe didn't let her out of his sight as she got ointment and clean rags from the house. After tossing the corn knife far into the field, he unsaddled his horse and hobbled it in the corn. The moment she'd finished tending Blue Boy, Lafe slipped his hand under her arm, drawing her toward the house.

"All right, Christy. Time to keep your bargain."

"I'm married," she told him.

Lafe's eyes dilated, black covering the crystalline iris. "To the Irisher? He deserted?"

"No! He was home on furlough in April."

Lafe smiled enough to show small teeth. "I like to imagine a husband's face as I enjoy his wife. Dan's face is far from handsome now, but it would be beautiful to me if I could see it while he watched us."

Then they were in the house. He turned her hand to look at the livid scar on her wrist, brought it to his lips. "I was a boy when I marked you, Christy, but even then I dreamed about the things I'd do with you when I got the chance."

The odor of smoke clung to him—was that hint of burned flesh her imagination? His mouth seared her throat. She caught his hands as he began to undo the rest of the buttons.

"I . . . I'm going to have a baby."

He drew back as if she were suddenly filthy. Then his eyes narrowed. "You're not showing."

"I've missed. . . ."

He made a gesture of repulsion. "All that makes me sick. I'm not sure I believe you, either." He pondered, watching her.

Her heartbeat slowed. She felt like a hunted animal feigning death.

His pale eyes glinted as he laughed. "Perhaps I can make you lose it. Yes, if I can remember that's Dan's thing growing in you. A mare aborts if she's ridden too hard and long. Don't see why that shouldn't be true for a woman. Get me a drink first. Is there any coffee?"

"Only sassafras tea."

He made a face and turned to the water bucket.

As if offering a drink, Christy raised the dipper and sloshed it in his face, grabbing at the same time for one of his guns. With any other man, she thought she could survive rape like a maiming but not fatal accident. With Lafe, she'd rather die.

He bent her wrist till she had to drop the revolver. She fastened her teeth in his hand, tasted the salt of blood before he struck her so hard lights exploded in her head. Then, through a dizzy whirling, she heard the dogs and the sound of horses.

Catching up the gun from the floor, Lafe peered from the edge of the window. "Bill Anderson! Now we'll see, Christy, how he feels about you with his sister dead. If he still has a kindness for you and you have some for him, don't cry-baby. He's got a bunch with him, but I can certainly blast him before he finishes me."

"Miss Christy!"

It was Anderson's voice. She should hope they would kill each other, Lafe and Bill Anderson, who was now implacable, but she remembered the handsome young man she'd helped nurse back to health, the one whose hawk face softened as he spoke of Josie. She buttoned her dress, smoothed her hair, and stepped outside.

While his wild band kept their saddles, Anderson trailed

his reins in front of his black horse and strode toward the house. He motioned toward the dead hounds sprawled at the edge of the trampled, broken stalks.

"Had some trouble, Miss Christy?"

Lafe stepped around her. "My boys got a little out of hand, Bill. Didn't like the hounds baying at them."

"Looks like your horse hobbled out in what's left of the corn."

"Hell, Bill! This is war."

Anderson's face twisted. "Yeah. Yeah, it is." A red silk cord with many knots was looped around the crown of his black hat. What looked like human hair decorated either side of the headstall at the brow band of his bridle. "Where are your men, Lafe?"

"Headed for Tom Maddux's folks a few miles away."

"You can show us. Quantrill's orders are to gather all the men we can, and meet him down in Texas, paying our respects along the way to any bluebellies or Union militia we're strong enough to tackle."

Lafe stiffened. Then he looked at the fifty or sixty guerrillas and gave a short laugh. "Fine. Texas ought to be a warmer place to spend the winter." He bowed to Christy. "Thanks for the drink. Sorry we can't visit longer about old times." He strolled toward his horse.

Anderson's blue gaze searched Christy. "Are you . . . hurt?"

"Not really. If you'll take him with you. . . ."

"You bet I will." Anderson hitched a shoulder. "I'd kill him for what he did to your corn and hounds, but we need him. He's the devil in a fight, and smart. Helped Quantrill plan the Lawrence raid."

This guerrilla had shot down helpless men, some in their doorways like her father, yet something in his eyes made her ache for him. "Mister Anderson, I . . . I'm sorry about Josie."

A muscle jerked in his cheek. "You're lucky you look like her, and that you saved my life." He swallowed. "Good bye, Christy Ware. I doubt we'll see each other again in this world."

"Good bye, Bill Anderson." She rose on tiptoe and kissed him for his dead sister.

He gave her a startled look—half of a wry smile—caught up the reins, and mounted. Lafe fell in beside him. In minutes they passed out of sight along the creek.

CHAPTER NINE

Christy began to shake. Her knees gave way. She sank down on the step, burying her face in her arms and wept for Lawrence, the widows and orphans there, wept for Josie and the dead young girls, for Mary Anderson who might never walk, wept with fresh pain for her father.

Blue Boy limped up with the other dogs that made soft mourning sounds as they pressed against her. She was caressing them, thankful that at least they were alive, when Sarah arrived.

Digging a grave deep and wide enough for ten animals in the rocky soil was such a formidable task that, instead, they pushed and pulled the wheelbarrow, laden with several hounds at a time, to a gully in the pasture, lowered them gently, and shoveled in earth from the banks.

"I want to tell Lige they weren't torn up and eaten," Sarah muttered through her tears. She and Christy rolled big rocks over the burial, held each other a while and sobbed. "Do you think your father would mind . . . would you . . . if I buried old Sam beside him?" Sarah asked. "Lige thought a lot of your father. It'd make him feel better about Sam when he comes homes . . . if he does."

"Father liked dogs. He'd be glad to have Sam close to him."

When the old hound was curled for his long sleep in the rich earth by Jonathan Ware's stone, Christy and Sarah bowed their heads. After a time, they studied the field.

Here and there, an ear of corn stood on an unbroken stalk. There were probably more, hidden by the shattered plants, but most of the crop had been stolen or wasted. Outrage smoldered in Christy as they washed blood from the wheelbarrow, tilted it to dry, and began the pitiful harvest. Nearly all guerrillas—most soldiers, for that matter— were farm boys, who had stumbled to bed worn out from plowing or chopping weeds away from the corn. Yet, in ten minutes, they had destroyed the reward of months of work. But considering the bloody harvest they'd reaped in Lawrence, it was lucky they hadn't fired the house. And Christy was lucky, so lucky, Bill Anderson had come to say good bye.

"Seed corn and a little to eat. We'll get quite a bit of fodder from the stalks," Sarah said, rubbing her back as she appraised the good corn in the wheelbarrow and the heap of ears beside it that had been smashed into the earth or partly crushed by hoofs or boots. Seed could be gleaned from them. "At least we grew some corn in the valley, but we'll have to gather all the nuts and wild fruit we can. With Hildy gone to Justus, there's one less mouth to feed, but one less woman to help, and Hildy was good help." Sarah looked straight at Christy. "Are you going to tell Hester about Lafe?"

"No, nor the others, either. They'll have to know guerrillas came and took the corn, but there's no use grieving Hester."

Sarah nodded. "Maybe we should dig the potatoes and get them to the valley before someone steals them." She frowned. "What with bushwhackers and soldiers after Quantrill, we might better stay in the valley."

It made sense. Christy didn't think there could be anyone as cruel as Lafe Ballard, but there might be. Yet glancing from her father's grave to the house, she felt that abandoning them was giving up all he had stood for, all she believed in, all she wanted to save for Dan, and surrendering to the evil of men like Lafe and Quantrill, Jennison, and the Red Legs.

"I can't leave, Sarah. But you don't have to stay."

"Of course I do!" Sarah gave her an exasperated hug. "I guess I know what you mean. The house stands for when neighbors helped each other, instead of killing them. It stands for the good ways we hope there'll be again . . . school and Sunday meetings, quilting, trading work, opening your door to strangers and giving them your best because that's how it should be, not because there's a gun at your head."

"Sarah. . . ."

Frowning at the row of bee gums ranged on stumps between the small orchard and the garden, Sarah turned with an exultant laugh. "There's bound to be some thieves want our honey. I just thought of a way to fix them good! We'll loop a rope around the bottom of each bee gum, so they're all connected. Then we'll tie on pieces of rope, hiding it in the grass, till the end reaches the dogtrot. . . ."

"And a yank on it will turn over the bee gums!" Christy finished for her.

"Yes. When my bees get after them, they'll skedaddle, whether they're bushwhackers, jayhawks, or soldiers. I hate to upset my bees, but it's better than the rascals making off with all their honey so they'd starve this winter."

Sarah could work around the bees without getting stung, so she tied the rope around the bee gums. Christy ran it behind the woodpile on the dogtrot and left the knotted end where it could be jerked without the perpetrator being seen.

The rest of the day, they dug potatoes, wheelbarrowed the sacks to the creek, and carried them to store inside the cave till Lad and Lass could take them through the passage. No more than a week's supply of potatoes would go in the root cellar, with a similar amount of turnips.

Next morning they were shaking plump brown potatoes loose from earth and plants when a wagon clattered out of the woods on the west. Relieved at the sunbonnets of driver and passenger, and recognizing Zephyr and Breeze stepping smartly along, Christy and Sarah went forward to meet Susie McHugh and Harriet Parks.

Their somber faces were not due entirely to the butchery at Lawrence. "That dreadful Jim Lane's been tearing around, working people up to cross into Missouri and serve the border counties as Lawrence was . . . burn, kill, get back stolen property and a lot more, besides." Susie shook her head. "Lawrence is in all the Northern papers, New York, Boston, Chicago . . . everywhere. You know, Lawrence was settled almost ten years ago by the New England Emigrant Aid Society, which was determined to make Kansas a free state. Most of the murdered men have friends and family back East. Money's pouring in to rebuild Lawrence, and the North's calling for vengeance, especially since Quantrill holds a Confederate commission and the raid's being praised in Southern papers."

"They're remembering the Red Legs and jayhawkers." Not much else could have been expected, but Christy's heart sank. "Is Jim Lane in Missouri?"

"General Ewing stopped him," Harriet said. "But he had to promise Lane that the Army would clear everybody out of the Missouri border counties so the guerrillas can't find shelter and support."

"Everybody?" Christy repeated.

"Everybody." Susie fumbled for a paper, then she handed it to Christy. "I made a copy of Order Number Eleven for you from the one sent Captain Wright, who's in command of the soldiers at Trading Post."

The words danced crazily as Christy tried to understand, reading snatches aloud: " 'August Twenty-Third, Eighteen Sixty-Three . . . All persons living in Jackson, Cass, and Bates

County, Missouri and that part of Vernon County included in this district, except those living within one mile of the limits of Independence, Hickman's Mills, Pleasant Hill, and Harrisonville, and except those in Kaw township . . . embracing Kansas City and Westport, are hereby ordered to remove from their places of residence within fifteen days. . . .' "

Skimming ahead, Christy summed it up for Sarah before giving her the paper. "People who can convince the commanding officer of the nearest station that they're loyal to the Union will get a certificate allowing them to move to any military station in the district or anywhere in Kansas except the border counties. Everyone else must leave the district."

Sarah read angrily: " 'All hay or grain in the field or under shelter . . . within reach of the military stations . . . will be taken to such stations . . . specifying the names of all loyal owners and the amount of such produce taken from them. All grain and hay . . . not convenient to such stations will be destroyed.' "

She and Christy looked toward the ravaged corn. "I don't know if it's better or worse to have your corn taken by the Army instead of bushwhackers," Christy said. "Lafe Ballard and Tom Maddux were through here with a gang yesterday. Killed most of the hounds and stole the corn."

The visitors' eyes widened as they looked more closely at the field. "Papa will give you some corn," Susie assured them.

"We have a little, and enough for seed," demurred Christy. "There are going to be people who need it a lot worse than we do when Missouri Unionists start crossing the line. As if a government voucher's going to feed them when their crops are lost! I'm glad Thos and Dan and Davie aren't stationed where they'd have to do such rotten work."

"Captain Wright's a decent man," Susie comforted.

"He's from Mound City and met your father at the mill. He knows Dan from riding with Montgomery."

"He has his orders." Christy gazed at the house, the giant walnut, so dear, and dearer still because of her father's death and these years she'd struggled to protect it. "Are . . . are they supposed to burn the buildings?"

Susie brightened a little. "General Schofield, who commands the Department of Missouri, won't approve the burning of property, and he and Ewing have issued strict orders that neither Kansas nor Missouri militia can cross the border without direct command from Ewing. Neither can groups of armed civilians on any pretext whatever."

"Order Eleven's hard and cruel," said Harriet. "But everyone says it's merciful compared to what Lane's thousands and the Red Legs would have done."

"That's not much comfort, but at least, thanks to you, we know what to expect." Christy wiped her hands on her apron. "Come in and have some tea."

"We'd better get back," Harriet said. "Mama gets cranky with the children, if she has to look after them very long." She sighed. "I wish she'd go live with one of her darling sons. She and Catriona are always bickering."

"Papa's certainly never going to marry her," Susie declared. "Christy, Sarah, we brought the wagon to help you move, in case any of you want to come stay with us. I'm sure we can persuade Captain Wright to look the other way."

"Unless Trav . . . I mean, the father of little Noelle . . . comes to get Lilah, I wouldn't be surprised if she stays with Star even after the war. Hester seems happy as long as she has Richie." A lump rose in Christy's throat as she looked at the house. "If . . . if I can't stay here, I'll go to the valley."

"So will I," said Sarah.

They waved the two women out of sight, looked at each

other wordlessly, and went back to digging potatoes.

Two days later, a squad of mounted men behind him, Captain Wright explained Order Number 11, looking as unhappy as if he were being exiled. His mild brown eyes avoided the women's. "I've already signed your certificates, Missus O'Brien, Missus Morrow. Since the order requires signatures of people affirming your loyalty, Missus Nickel and the Parkses gave theirs." He tugged ferociously at his flowing moustache. "I regret this, ladies, especially since your husbands are both Union soldiers. To some degree, it's for your own safety. General Ewing fears when the guerrillas' families are forced to leave, the devils will take vengeance on any Union folks left in the district."

Sarah thinned her shapely nose. "This feels like vengeance!" She stalked toward the house.

"There's no corn for you to take," said Christy. "The guerrillas helped themselves."

"You don't seem to have any animals except the dogs."

"We don't have as many as we did before the guerrillas hit four days ago."

Captain Wright blushed. "I'm sorry . . . they dodged our patrol."

Christy showed him a little mercy. "They crossed farther north."

"Good. I mean . . . it's not good they crossed, but. . . ." He floundered. "I hope it'll cheer you to know that Fort Smith fell to the Union again. This time, we'll keep it. All Stand Watie and his Indians can hope to do now is raid supply wagons along the Military Road. We will win, Missus O'Brien, and then. . . ."

There was sudden commotion, crashing, and shrieks. Christy and Wright whirled to see three of his men bolting for the creek, covering their faces, slapping wildly at bees swarming out of overturned beehives.

Two of the soldiers dived in the creek, but the third tripped on a log and went sprawling. A fresh scream burst from him. He sat up, swatting at the bees, but he couldn't get to his feet.

Sarah, coming out from behind the woodpile, ran till she began to encounter angry bees and slowed to a walk. She wafted her skirts carefully around the soldier who had buried his face in his arms. The bees hovered. Then their buzzing numbers, including those that had pursued their molesters to the water, began to drift back to their toppled hives.

By the time Christy and Wright approached, Sarah was slapping mud on the soldier's hands, head, face, and neck.

"My leg!" he moaned.

"Let it be a lesson to you, Hawkins. No foraging except by order." Wright's tone was severe, but he was gentle as he slit the boy's pant leg with his pocket knife.

No bones protruded, but there was a deformity under the skin, and, when Hawkins stirred, there was a sound of bone grinding on bone. "Any of you men know how to set a broken leg?" the captain yelled.

No one did. Sarah bit her lip, peering at the injury. "I helped Lige set his leg when it was broken about like this," she said. "He gripped hard below his knee, and I pulled from just above the ankle till the broken edges separated and could be eased back together. I padded boards and bandaged them on each side to keep the bones straight. Healed just fine."

Young Hawkins's blue eyes fixed on her from a mud plaster, only a few strands of chick-yellow hair escaping. "Would . . . would you help me, ma'am? I was just so hungry for some honeycomb. . . ."

"Will you hold his leg below the knee, Captain?" Sarah asked. "Christy, will you find some boards and something to pad and bandage with?"

Two soldiers squatted at the creekbank, daubing mud on their stings. As Christy ran to the house, a grizzled older man passed her with a flask. "A good slug of whiskey'll help the boy. Maybe the cap'n won't romp me too hard for breakin' rules and havin' a mite along for my rheumatiz."

Cloth was more precious than ever, now there was no wool, and, concentrating on food crops, they hadn't been growing cotton or flax. Christy's dress was patched in a dozen places. She'd make up the beautiful blue gingham Dan had brought this winter, but she'd save it for his next visit—or homecoming!—as long as she could. Good thread was unraveled, to be woven again, but the ragbag held enough worn-out scraps for padding. The middle cut from an old sheet could bind in place shelves she took from the well house.

When the leg was set and held in place by boards well padded and bandaged, one of the squad approached. "Shall we rig a litter, Cap'n?"

Wright scowled. "Four miles of that would jar him plenty. Best thing is for some of you to ride back and fetch a wagon . . . with lots of featherbeds!"

"Why not leave him here?" Christy began. Then she remembered. September 9th, ten days from now, was when she and Sarah were supposed to be gone. The captain turned red, but suddenly his mild features perked up.

"You'd look after him?"

"Of course we would, but. . . ."

"If any of our men are wounded or fall sick while patrolling this region, would you take care of them?"

Christy caught in her breath at the glimmer of hope.

"We would. We've nursed a man with an ugly bullet wound and know something of healing herbs."

"I reckon I have some discretion," Wright said. "Sure seems useful to me to have a place this side of the border where our soldiers can be looked after." He glanced at his men. "I'll argue this with General Ewing himself, if I have to, boys, but I don't see why anyone but us needs to know."

There was general nodding and approving murmurs. While Sarah and Christy hurried to fix a bed, four of the men carried Hawkins to the house. Before they brought him in, Sarah cleaned the mud off him and replaced it with dock root ointment that she passed around to the other afflicted soldiers.

Hawkins's bedroll and pack was brought from his saddle, and his blanket spread to protect the sheets. "I'll send over his rations," said Wright while friends took off Hawkins's boots and outer clothing. "I'm mightily obliged."

He took the certificates and scribbled notes on each. "There. Says you're hereby charged with nursing and sheltering Union soldiers who require such aid. Since my command's responsible for this section, you shouldn't have any trouble with our soldiers, but, if you do, send them to me."

Sarah and Christy said as one: "Thank you, Captain."

He grinned, plainly as relieved as they were. "We'll take Hawkins's horse with us, just in case a thief happens along, but a man'll bring it for him when he's able to ride."

As Wright and his band rode off, Sarah eyed the youthful invader of her hives. "I'm going to set up the bee gums again, and tell my bees it's all right. If they let me take some honeycomb for you, will you promise never to steal from a hive again?"

"But we keep bees at home, ma'am. Mama takes care of them."

"She always leaves them plenty for winter?"

"Oh yes, ma'am. She's real careful about taking honey. Won't let the rest of us come nigh. And she plants all kinds of flowers they like."

"Then I'm surprised you didn't know better."

He squirmed. "Mama'd give me a hiding, if she'd seen me. But I could just taste honeycomb, ma'am. And . . . oh, I don't know, when you're a soldier, even militia like us, and a bunch of you are out somewhere. . . ."

"You do things you wouldn't if you were home."

"I'm afraid that's about the size of it, ma'am."

He looked very young. The swellings puffed out his round, freckled face even more, and his body hadn't caught up with his gangling arms and legs. "Don't call me 'ma'am'. I'm Sarah and this is Christy. Who are you?"

"Will Hawkins, ma . . . I mean, Miss Sarah. From south of Mound City."

"How old are you?"

He crimsoned. "Fifteen."

"They take boys that young in the militia?"

"Bushwhackers kill us for men," he retorted. " 'Most all the soldier-age men in Kansas joined the Army a long time ago, so the militia can't be choosy. Anyhow, I said I was eighteen, and Mama signed for me."

"I hope she's got sons at home with better sense."

"Matt's twelve and Billy's fourteen. My big brother Harry lost an arm at Pea Ridge, but he's learned to do most anything."

"Where's your father?"

"He . . . well, he got himself killed at Pea Ridge along with my Uncle Bax."

This was what it meant for just one family when it said 1,384 Union men were lost in that battle. A father and husband and kinsman dead, a son and brother maimed for life. If the war ground on, besides Will, there were two more boys who might be harvested long before their season.

Look at Mrs. Nickel: of her sons who saw their cabin burned by Clarke's marauders seven years ago, six were in the Army as well as her tall, golden-haired husband. Who would be left when it was over?

"I'll get you some honeycomb," Sarah told the boy.

"I'm going to the Hayes tannery," Christy said. "Allie will have to move. I'm afraid she doesn't have anywhere to go."

Sarah raised an eyebrow. "Do you think . . . ?"

"I don't know. I'll ask in the valley before I go see her."

Hester Ballard vouched for Allie as being a good woman, and Christy described all the help Ethan and Allie Hayes had given her family when they first moved here. "Mary and Beth were great friends," she said, and then frowned. "The two older boys are in the Army, but Luke may still be home, helping his mother. He's fifteen."

"He should not come here." Star's tone was positive. "He is of wants to be a warrior age, and is bound to go soon. Better he not know about the valley. But his mother and sister are welcome."

Lilah nodded. Matured by motherhood, she was so lovely that Christy thought Travis Jardine, if he ever saw them again, would have to want to take care of her and sweet little Noelle.

"I'll see what I can do," Christy promised. "Thank you, Star."

Star chuckled. "I was surely wrong when I thought I would live alone all the rest of my life."

Allie Hayes was thirty-nine, four years younger than

Ellen Ware, but she looked the older now, yellow hair streaked with white, sun wrinkles at eyes and mouth, beginning to stoop from labor. Only her brilliant blue eyes were the same. They sparkled with angry tears as she gestured at her cornfield.

"That jumped-up Captain Wright's sending a wagon and men to take my corn on the Ninth, and Mary and me have to be gone by then! Where and how, I'd like to know? Nora Caxton's already gone to live with her sister in Springfield and the Madduxes still have a team and wagon and enough money for the train or steamboat, but how'm I supposed to get back to Kentucky, where we came from when we first got married? I haven't heard from any of our folks since the war began. Luke took our old mule when he headed for Arkansas to join up with Pap Price and find his brothers and pa. When he came by here last week, Lafe Ballard stole our last critter, a runty hog."

Mary, at nine, leggy and reaching to Allie's breast, hugged her mother around the waist and tried to pat her cheek. "We can walk, Mama. We've fed lots of people and let them sleep in our house or barn. I bet there's plenty of folks'll do the same for us. . . ."

"Won't be anybody left till we get to the south end of Vernon County, and not many after that all the way down through Arkansas, where there's been so much fighting." She brooded, holding Mary close. "What makes it worse is half the men in Wright's bunch, includin' him, have brought hides to the tannery for years. They know us."

Christy remembered Watt Caxton shooting down her father. "That's what makes it so awful."

Allie reached for her hand. "I'm afraid I haven't been much of a neighbor these last years, Christy. Seems like I haven't had time to breathe since Ethan and Matt left, and then Mark. Still, I'd've got over, someway, if I hadn't known Sarah was with you, and Hester." She gave a wan smile. "I heard you married Dan O'Brien. Always liked that lad, and could he fiddle! I hope he'll come home safe to you."

"And I hope Ethan and your boys will."

"It don't seem right that you and Sarah have to leave, too, when your men are in the Union Army. Reckon you'll go to Kansas."

Christy gazed at Allie and tried to gauge if she could be trusted, if she could fit in with Lilah and Star.

"How's little Beth?" Allie asked. "She must miss your mama, who I hear tell has gone to be a nurse. She can be right proud of doing that. Only thing I've got to brag on is how I kept the jayhawks from stealing our lard last year." Allie grinned. "The captain was having it loaded when I said . . . 'Oh, well, it would've been a shame to make it into soap.' He said that would be a terrible waste, and I said . . . 'To be sure, sir, but the hog had cholera.' " Allie laughed hugely. "He thought I might be lying, but he didn't dare chance it. I didn't let you say, though . . . how is Beth?"

"Beth's fine." Allie would never do anything to hurt Beth—any child. "Allie, if . . . if there were a place close by where you could stay, would you do it till the war's over?"

"A place to hide?"

Christy nodded.

"Honey," said Allie with fervor, "I'd live in a cave if I could be around when my men come home."

Christy burst out laughing. "You won't have to live in a cave now," she said, and told them.

CHAPTER TEN

A son! He, Daniel Patrick O'Brien, whose birth family had long since returned to the sod of County Clare, had a son in this new world, born of his beloved. Even if he died, part of him would live in the child who'd claim his share of joy, grief, work, and rewards in the country Dan fought for.

Jon's hair is between yours and mine, Christy wrote. *I'm sending you a curl. It's much the color of Father's, rich red-brown, and lots of it, but he's going to have your eyes, Danny, hazy gray like autumn mist on the hills. Beth and Mary won't let him whimper for more than a second when we're in the valley, so he keeps Sarah and me hopping when we're at the cabin. How I wish you could see him! How I wish I knew where you are! It's been a month since I had your letter saying you boys were fed up with guarding the road to the harbor there at Johnsonville and that you want to see more action. I can understand that you'd rather get hurt in a real battle, rather than be picked off by guerrillas, but, oh, my darling love, take care of yourself. Little Jon needs a father and you need him. Also, there's that little girl we both want, remember?*

I'm going to have all my babies the Osage way. It makes a lot better sense to be upright and hold onto willow posts to work with the baby. Star gave me cherry bark tea to help make the pains powerful enough, and, after Jon came, Hester gave me lots of fennel tea to make sure I had plenty of milk.

Star made him a pine cradleboard. You should see him watch a tail feather from the scarlet tanager that nests in our big tree, and the bright green parakeet feathers Richie found. The board's so convenient. I can carry Jon and have my hands free or can prop him against something or even hang him from a tree. That sounds awful, but you know what I mean!

Dan held his son's bright curl to his cheek. It clung there, soft, finer than down. He wrapped it carefully in the envelope and put it in a lined oiled-silk bag he'd bought in St. Louis to hold such treasures. The letter was dated February 10, 1864. Because of the vagaries of military transport, after weeks of no mail, he'd had four letters from Christy that afternoon of April 13th, including one written the day of Jonathan Daniel's birth. He, Davie Parks, and Thos Ware got boxes, too, that day, but, although they'd existed that winter on the worst rations of Dan's entire time in the Army—hardtack and barreled salt pork with lean streaks turned a villainous green—they read their letters several times over before attacking the boxes with bayonets, purloined because they weren't supplied to artillerymen but made wonderful candle holders with the sharp end stuck in the ground and were generally a useful tool around camp. Soldiers hated to use bayonets for their real purpose and very seldom did, even under orders.

"If they have to dig through our boxes at regimental headquarters to make sure there's no whiskey, you'd think they could at least have a care about how they treat our things," Dan grumbled, using a pick to pry up the last nail from Christy's box. He had two more! One from the Parkses, and one from his mother-in-law who was nursing in Nashville, only eighty miles away. Several times he'd been granted a few days' furlough to ride the train to the city and visit her and Lydia, who was also there, looking almost pretty in spite of her exhausting work.

"It's plain craziness about the whiskey." Thos held up a wool shirt from his mother and admired it before unwrapping some chocolate and savoring it with his eyes closed. "Officers get all the commissary whiskey they can pay for anytime they want it. Plenty of them are drunk when they're giving orders that could get us killed, but an enlisted man can't buy a drop without a written order signed by his captain, and any sutler who sells spirits will lose his license."

"Ah, but look what my clever Peggy contrived, lads!" Harry Shepherd exhibited a big roasted turkey. His dark eyes glinted as he reached inside it and produced a corked bottle. "Peach brandy, bless my girl's heart! And here's spiced nuts, gingerbread, sausage, lean bacon, pickles, cheese!" His black eyebrows knitted. "But why did Peg send six pairs of socks?" He read a note and his grin faded. "She'd made three pair for Tim. Since he's gone, she wants me to give these and some of the goodies to soldiers who haven't got families to send them things."

Since it had been months since the battery got any boxes, most men received at least one as the wagon was unloaded. The half dozen or so who got nothing watched the joyful unpacking wistfully or moped off to their tents.

"We'll all share." Davie put a ham on the lid and unwrapped socks and a warm shirt from around jars of preserves and relish. "Look! Susie's made my favorite black walnut applesauce cake! Catriona sent currant scones . . . Harriet put in gingersnaps and caramels . . . Missus Morrison did nice big handkerchiefs . . . and Papa's sent two books . . . George Borrow's *Wild Wales* and Palgrave's *Golden Treasury*! And there's potatoes, onions, and apples tucked in every place one'll fit, and dried apple and pear slices in any little chink!" A smaller box from his big sister Lydia contained envelopes, writing paper, needles, and thread to share with Dan. Dan got the same delicious edibles from his foster sisters, as well as sewing needs, a shirt, and chocolate from Mrs. Ware who'd asked him to please call her Ellen. But it was Christy's box that made his eyes blur.

She must have unraveled her best shawl to make the soft muffler, mittens, and socks. The picture of her doing that by firelight, big with his child, wrenched his heart. He knew guerrillas had ruined or carried off the corn, but a note explained she had devised the fruit bars with ground nut meal, more nuts, applesauce, currants, and honey. Pear, peach, and grape leathers or dried apple and persimmon slices were wedged into every possible space. Honeycomb from Sarah Morrow filled a jar sealed with beeswax. A large crock was jammed with pickled eggs and a smaller crock held butter. From Star there were cakes of maple sugar and candy of maple syrup boiled with all manner of nuts. Hester sent boneset leaves, ground coneflower root, and black haw bark for colds and flu, and, for enjoyment, a tea of fragrant crumbled sassafras bark and spicebush. Lilah's petticoat must have supplied three finely stitched handkerchiefs with his initials embroidered in a corner. Beth had drawn a creditable likeness of Jon in his cradleboard, and written proudly that she would help him learn to walk. There were notes and pictures from Richie and Mary Hayes. Dan was touched to have them, even if they were "school" assignments. Since Ellen had left, Star, Sarah, and Christy were teaching the children, along with Lilah and Hester, who were learning to read and write.

After the bounty was shared with men who'd got no boxes, Dan's mess—Shepherd, Thos, and Davie—had a banquet.

"I'm glad we got potatoes," Shepherd said as he fried some in butter. "When we're guarding the supply route for the Army of the Cumberland, you'd think the quartermaster could give us some fruit and vegetables, so we won't all come down with scurvy. Five men have it so bad, they've been sent to the Nashville hospital."

Happily replete, the battery boys lounged from tent to tent that night, joking and exchanging choice viands. The commander's sister was visiting with her baby, a winsome lass of less than two years, whose golden hair shone from beneath the red hood of her cloak as her mother sat with her on a box outside their tent. Her name was Annie and she laughed and reached for the faces of the men who crowded around to see her.

We serenaded her with "Annie Laurie". She laughed and called us "nice, pretty so-jers," bless her heart. Her father, a captain like her uncle, is stationed in Nashville. Seeing such a darling little colleen made us almost as happy as getting our boxes. Dan wrote by candlelight in the Sibley tent his gun crew shared. These twelve feet high, teepee-like shelters had passed out of official use two years ago because the iron tripods that held them up were heavy and cumbersome to transport, but the quartermaster had located some for the long-encamped battery. Each was supposed to shelter twelve men, so the nine of them almost had enough room. The cone-shaped stove was useless for cooking and not much better for heat till Shepherd thought of building a little oven of bricks and setting the stove on top to serve as part of the chimney. The stove pipe supplied by the quartermaster was too short to reach the top of the tent, so the men chipped in to buy enough pipe to vent the smoke outside.

All our crew got boxes and are writing home tonight before we turn in like spokes on a wheel with our feet to the stove and our heads to the canvas. Usually Davie reads anything he can find, Thos plays checkers with Mac Ford or Harry Shepherd, and the rest play cards or smoke their pipes and tell yarns. Tonight,

*though, we're all scribbling away to finish our letters before
"Taps".*

He would read her new bunch of letters till he had them
by heart, but now he glanced back through them quickly,
reading news he'd skipped the first time in order to find her
love words and how she and the baby were doing.

In a letter inexplicably delayed since he'd had several
with later dates, she had written: *You'll have heard that
about 300 of Quantrill's men, some dressed in Federal uniforms,
attacked the little garrison at Baxter Springs, perhaps 100 black
and white soldiers, about noon, October 6th. The soldiers were
holding them off when the guerrillas galloped away. They'd
learned General Blunt was on his way to Fort Smith with eight
wagons, some ladies and civilians in buggies, a brass band—
mostly young German boys in brand new uniforms—and an escort of 100 men. Because of the stolen uniforms, Blunt thought
the Union garrison was coming to meet him. When the guerrillas
opened fire, Blunt's men were so startled that some ran. The officers rallied them when more Rebels burst out of the timber. Blunt
got the ladies to safety, but most of the escort were chased down
and shot even after surrendering. The bandwagon tried to get
away—the musicians weren't armed—but the youngsters were all
shot and the wagon set afire while some were still alive. Quantrill
rode on to Texas for the winter. We hope he won't be back.*

*You remember William Hairgrove who was terribly wounded
by Hamelton's gang in that gully above the Marais des Cygnes.
He's a soldier at Leavenworth now, though his hair's white and
he's old for the Army. Anyway, he found out that William Griffith, one of the murderers, was living across the river in Missouri. Griffith was arrested, tried in Mound City, and hanged.
Susie McHugh says everyone thinks he's the only one who'll
ever be punished, though surely some of them have been killed in
the war.*

An early February letter had happier tidings. *The Ladies Enterprise Society of Mound City has organized to build a meeting house. They give glorious suppers to raise money and have musical evenings, plays, and lectures that the soldiers stationed there are glad to support. There's a singing school, children's classes, and the United Brethren, Baptists, Methodists, and Presbyterians each have a day to hold services. It would be heaven if you were stationed that close, but surely the war can't last too much longer, can it, Danny?*

He had already written her of his high hopes once General Grant was put in command of all Union forces April 4th. *What it amounts to, darling, is the Union controls the Mississippi and everywhere west of it except for the Confederate forces left in Arkansas and Indian Territory. Grant can get more men and supplies. The South's running out of both. Grant hopes to break Lee's Army in Virginia and have Sherman and the other Union generals push east to the ocean.*

"Taps" sounded, that poignant, most beautiful of all camp melodies. Dan put his letters and writing things in his knapsack, nestled Jon's fiery curl with Christy's black one in the silver snuff box he'd bought to keep the precious lock from getting lost or dirty, and blew out his candle. Except in the bitterest weather, he stripped to his underwear before rolling up in Christy's blanket. He tucked the snuff box beneath the shirt he used for a pillow, imagined her asleep with their son nearby, and was soon asleep in spite of Shepherd's resonant snoring.

Word came next day of the slaughter of 238 Negro soldiers and many white ones at Fort Pillow, Tennessee. General Nathan Forrest's troops swarmed through, killing men who were trying to surrender. The river ran red with the blood of those shot while trying to escape.

"There won't be any Negroes surrender after this." Shepherd's tone was somber. "Of course, they've known all along that the Rebs'll most likely kill them when it's not possible to capture and sell them as slaves."

"Lincoln tried to put a stop to that," said Dan, "by ordering that a Rebel prisoner would be shot for every Union soldier killed contrary to the rules of war, and for each sold into slavery, a Rebel prisoner would be put at hard labor till the Union man was released. That probably kept the South from executing or selling the Fifty-Fourth Massachusetts men captured after their attack on Fort Wagner."

"Father doesn't believe in war at all." After more than two years, Davie still didn't look old enough to be a soldier. "But he says it's shameful that colored soldiers are paid only ten dollars a month to a white's thirteen, and then three dollars of that's held out for clothing, so they only get seven dollars."

"I'll bet Colonel Montgomery and the other white commanding officers are trying to change that," said Dan. "For that matter, boys, have you heard we may get a pay raise?"

"I'll believe it when I see it!" snorted Shepherd.

At the end of April, Captain Tenney had official business at Waverly, an outpost ten miles from the river. The road wound through thick timber, the sort guerrillas liked, so the captain was escorted by twenty men, including Dan and Davie, mounted on battery horses and armed with Colt revolvers.

It was the kind of spring morning that proclaims with moist earth smells, birdsong, and fresh leaf that winter is over. Raven pranced a bit, although he was getting old for a battery horse. After Dan married, he'd had two-thirds of his pay sent to Christy, in care of Uncle Simeon, but he was saving all he could with the hope of buying Raven when the war ended, or if the horse became unfit for duty. They'd been through a lot since Dan first harnessed the big black horse at Leavenworth two years ago. Two years, and Dan had been in the Army almost a year before that. Close to three years of his twenty-four spent in this war.

The captain and riders in front stopped to let their mounts drink from a stream flowing across the road. Suddenly shots hummed around the escort.

"Up ahead, men!" yelled Captain Tenney. "Take cover behind that ridge!"

Gaining the other side of the rocky spine, Rebels whooping after them, they flung themselves from their horses and knelt where they could steady their pistols and aim at the oncoming band of wild-looking men armed with muskets, squirrel rifles, and shotguns.

By a miracle, no soldier seemed to be seriously hurt, but one horse lay quietly in the stream, and another thrashed on the bank, screaming, till it gave a final convulsion and its head dropped.

"Make your bullets count, boys!" called Tenney. "We're almost as many as they are! They didn't count on a fight. Let's give them one!"

A shot whipped off the hat of a gray-coated man in the lead, baring his golden hair. *The color of Richie's,* Dan thought with a pang. Although his scar smoldered and the man was his best target, Dan aimed at the raggedy knees of a wiry, bearded fellow in the act of firing his musket. Dan missed. Someone else didn't. The man dropped his weapon, threw up his arms, half turned, and fell.

Dan eared back the hammer and fired at a redhead in a greasy vest. He yelped, clapped his hand over his bleeding thigh, and staggered into the brush as the others were

166

doing, except for three sprawled bodies and a man with sunny hair who moaned as he pressed his hands over a wound in his belly. Blood leaked through his fingers to dribble to the ground.

Davie gripped Dan's arm, jerked his head toward the wounded enemy. "I shot him! I . . . I did that!"

"He was after us." Dan dropped a bracing hand on the boy's shoulder. "Look, Davie, you've been on a gun crew for two years. . . ."

"Yes," whispered Davie. "But I was never sure we'd hit anyone."

"If we didn't, lad, we've wasted a great lot of shell and powder," Dan said, and turned to his brother-in-law. "Thos, looks like you'll have a permanent part on the left side. Here, let me bandage it. My handkerchief's cleaner than yours."

When Dan turned back, he saw Davie kneeling by the blond Rebel, offering his canteen.

A swift glance must have assured the captain that his soldiers were all fit to ride. "Mount up, men!" Tenney called. "Take turns riding with the two who lost horses." He wiped his forehead and settled his hat more firmly. "We gave those gentlemen more than they reckoned on. I'll bet we've seen the last of them for today." Tenney scowled at the fallen guerrillas. "Guess we shouldn't leave them for the hogs. Who'll volunteer for burial detail?"

"Davie and I will," Dan said. "Shall we rig a litter for the wounded one?"

Tenney rode over to stare at the Rebel. "Gut-shot. No use jouncing him along."

"Be a mercy to shoot him in the head," Shepherd muttered.

Davie looked up. His face was tear-streaked. "I've told him I'll stay with him."

Tenney considered. He must have sensed that no order would make Davie budge. "All right, then, Parks, O'Brien. Catch up as soon as you can."

It was only then that Dan saw blood trickling from a wound in Raven's shoulder. The dead Rebels wouldn't need their shirts; he'd use some of their clothing to make a dressing and bandage. On his way to the bodies, he paused beside the man in the gray coat. From the intricate knots of tarnished gold braid above the cuffs and the gold star on each lapel, Dan knew he must have once been a major in the regular Army, or had stolen the coat from one.

Davie cradled the golden head, speaking so softly that Dan caught only a few words. " 'Yea, though I walk through the valley of the shadow of death, I will fear no evil . . . for thou art with me. . . .' "

That face! For a horrible moment, Dan went dizzy as Richie's six-year-old features masked the dying Rebel's. He remembered Hildy's saying Richie had an older brother in school, in Boston, when the war broke out.

"Frazer?"

Blue eyes opened. "How'd you . . . know . . . ?"

"If you have a little brother named Richie, he's safe with good people who love him."

Sweat dewed Frazer's pallid forehead. "Thanks, Yank," he panted. He tried to lift a bloody hand, but it dropped again, exposing the top of a gold signet ring. "Give Richie . . . love and . . . ring. . . ."

"We'll take care of him," Dan promised.

He hurried to strip shirts from the nearest dead men and ran back to Raven. Fixing a pad in place with the sleeves and strips of torn shirt tied together to make a bandage, he was making a final knot when the *crack* of a shot was followed by a cry.

He whirled to see Davie collapse over Frazer, the ring glinting as it slipped from his grasp. A colored man dragged himself out of the trees, leaving a trail of blood, dropping a musket in order to crawl more swiftly to the bodies.

"Robbin' the wounded!" he snarled at Davie, and shoved his limp form off Frazer's. "Oh, Lordy, Master Edmund! What they done to you?"

Dan had his revolver cocked, but, when he understood the servant's mistake, he couldn't kill him. There wasn't any need. Pink foam bubbled from the Negro's mouth. He huddled against Frazer's side and didn't speak again.

Dan dropped beside Davie, frantically seeking a faint breath, the dimmest heartbeat. There was none. A bullet had crashed through the back of the head to burst out the left temple. It must have plowed crossways right through Davie's brain.

And Frazer was still alive. Again his face changed, narrowed, developed a cleft in the chin. Gold hair paled to silver, blue eyes faded to mocking crystal.

Dan's cheek throbbed, stung as if gunpowder was again being ground into his raw flesh. He leveled the Colt. Then it was once more Frazer who watched him. Dan shuddered and thrust the revolver into its holster as he took Davie's place, pillowing Frazer's head, holding one gory hand. Frazer had fumbled the other so that it rested on his servant's head.

Through the tightness in his throat, Dan said: "Since Davie can't, friend, I'll stay with you."

Frazer's eyes thanked him. The light was fading from their blue depths when two Rebels came out of the brush and blazed away at Dan.

Dan roused to the *creak* and jolting of a wagon. His leg

hurt like fury, his head, bandaged, felt as if it would split, his upper right arm ached, and the forearm was bent and bandaged to his chest. Beside him, blood had soaked through the blanket wrapped around what must be the mortal remnant of Davie.

Two black ears caught the edge of Dan's vision. He looked higher and sighed with relief. Good old Raven, following along, not limping much.

"You back with us?" Harry Shepherd leaned from the driver's place on the board seat. "When we heard a shot, we headed back. Then we heard more shots. Got there just as a bushwhacker was fixing to blow off your head at close range."

"We borrowed the wagon at a farm," explained Thos. "Captain Tenney detailed us and half the escort to get you to camp and send you on to the Nashville hospital on the next train. Your skull's so thick the bullet bounced off the side of it, and the bullet went clear through your arm, so the surgeon won't be probing around with his filthy hands to get the bullet out. Your leg bones are all busted up, though. Damned Miniés. . . ."

Fear twisted Dan's guts worse than he had felt at sight of the bushwhackers aiming at him before he could reach his Colt. He remembered the heaps of arms and legs he'd seen outside field hospitals, and broke out in cold sweat.

"I'm not going to let some damn' sawbones take off my leg!"

After a moment's silence, Thos leaned around to place a hand on Dan's shoulder. "They'll use chloroform. And Mother'll take care of you."

It wasn't the pain of amputation Dan shrank from, but afterward. He might have gotten along without an arm, but how could he plow and work cumbered by a crutch or wooden leg? He'd be a burden to Christy, not a help.

"Listen, boys," he said. "Leave a revolver under my mattress or pallet or whatever they lay me on."

Thos swung around. "Dan! You won't . . . ?"

"Oh, I won't kill myself." He forced a grin. "Just want something to fight off the surgeon, if he tries to chop me up in spite of what I say."

"All right," conceded Thos. "I'll leave you my Colt and use yours when I get back to camp."

"The things some fellows pull to get out of burial duty!" Shepherd said. "The other boys must still be digging graves for those six Rebs and the colored man." The joshing was meant to cheer him up, Dan knew, but he couldn't summon a chuckle. He hurt too much, and although he still couldn't believe Davie was dead, he knew he was.

If it would bring Davie back, Dan would let them take both legs. But it wouldn't. Nothing could. Uncle Simeon must mourn his youngest son, fruit of his mother's early death. Lydia, Susie, and Owen would weep for the brother they'd helped to raise. And Davie, so fresh and young and beautiful, would never exult in a girl's love, never have a child.

"Since Lydia's nursing in the city," said Thos, "we thought she'd want to get her brother ready to be buried and have the service there, where the grave will always be looked after."

"Yes," Dan managed. "That'll help the family . . . to know Lydia took care of him. . . ."

"There was a signet ring on the ground by the blond Reb," went on Shepherd. "We thought maybe it was something he'd asked you to send his folks, so we put it in your haversack."

Dan wasn't sure if he said—"Good."—or only tried to

before he lapsed into a stupor.

He roused at his own moaning when they lifted him out of the wagon, and again when he was carried to the train on a litter that Thos and Shepherd held by the ends that rested on feed sacks.

"Raven?" he muttered.

"We'll see to him," Shepherd promised. "The rest of our crew'll baby him till Thos and I get back."

The suspended litter swayed and jolted with the train's motion in spite of his friends' steadying hands, but it was a lot more comfortable than the wagon. When Dan next became fully aware, his nostrils tingled at a pungent odor. Someone was working on his wounded arm. Other gentle hands were busy at his leg. He gazed into the kind dark eyes and sweet face of Ellen Ware. She wore a brown dress over brown bloomers of the kind that had startled the neighbors of the Wattleses.

"You . . . you sure look better than any angel, Missus . . . I mean, Ellen." He couldn't keep the hot sting at the back of his eyelids from changing into tears, he was so happy to see her.

"I'm glad I'm here. I've always prayed that none of my boys be wounded, but if they were, that I could be with them."

Her boys? She truly ranked him with Thos and Charlie? Christy was his love, but she was not his mother, lost these many years. His heart expanded at Ellen's tenderness. Then, for the first time, he noticed something was gone.

His scar didn't burn! Not the slightest bit. There had been that moment when Edmund Frazer had turned into Lafe, one moment of furious searing, and then Lafe's mark

172

had tormented him no more. Warily he raised his good arm and ran his fingers over the wealed edges. It was just dead tissue. A scar that was finally healed. He then reached under the thin mattress. Thos hadn't failed him. The Colt was there.

Reassured, he glanced around and saw he had the corner bed in a long room with an aisle running between two rows of cots, ten on each side. The bandaged legs of several men were elevated by pulley affairs. The man next to Dan had a cloth-swathed stump of an arm. Beyond him, a gray-haired nurse changed dressings on one poor soul who had lost both legs at the thigh.

"Danny!" Lydia Parks moved into his range of vision. She bent and kissed him. "I . . . I'm glad you were with David. The shot must have killed him instantly, didn't it?"

"Yes." At least there was that comfort. Any Quaker would be proud of the way Davie had died. Summoning all his strength, Dan told her about the dying Rebel. "The strangest thing of all is that he was little Richie's brother. I've got his ring. Maybe you'd send it to Christy when you write." He glanced ruefully at his wounded arm.

"I'll write for you," Ellen promised.

"Thos brought David's books and things," said Lydia. "I'll send those home, too." Grief contorted her thin face. "Poor Father! He loves us all, but David was the apple of his eye." She turned away, shoulders heaving.

Ellen slipped an arm around her. "It'll help your father and family to know that you got David ready for burial. He'll have a marker. His grave will be tended, not like so many lonely ones grown over with weeds."

"I know." Lydia wiped her eyes. "And I'm thankful my brother died helping a man, rather than in the act of killing." With obvious effort, she composed herself and took

Dan's hand. "Surgeon Townsend is extremely skillful, dear. We're not getting new battle victims now, so he's not rushed and can take every precaution. . . ."

"Not with me!" At the women's shocked faces, Dan spoke more calmly. "If I were a teacher or merchant or something where I could earn my family's living with one leg, I guess I'd let the surgeon take the other one." He clamped his teeth till he had control of his voice. "All I know is farming. I'll go home able to take care of Christy or I won't go home at all."

"Dan," entreated Lydia, "Christy wouldn't want that! She'd feel like Colonel Montgomery's wife, who told Susie, if they shot off both her husband's arms and legs, she still wanted him home so she could take care of him."

"I doubt he'd want it!" Dan retorted. "Anyhow, they've been married a long time and have children old enough to do the farm work. If I die of this leg, Christy'll find a good man after a while."

"I doubt she will," said Ellen of her daughter.

"At least," said Dan grimly, "I won't be in her way."

The surgeon came in, a robust graying man in a once-white linen duster. Two soldiers followed him with a litter. "Awake, are we, Corporal?" he boomed. His light brown eyes swept Dan from head to foot. "The arm, nurse?" he asked Ellen.

"The ball passed through, Doctor Townsend. I cleaned the wound and dressed it with lint soaked in turpentine."

"That should do finely." The surgeon drew back the sheet and examined Dan's leg. "Sorry, my boy. We'll have to take it off." He motioned to the stretcher-bearers.

"No," said Dan.

Townsend gave an impatient sigh. "Corporal, the middle third of your left tibia and fibula are fractured and extensively comminuted. Gangrene or pyæmia is almost certain."

"I'll take that chance, sir."

The surgeon chewed his lip. "If you're set on trying to save the leg, I might perform a linear incision along the inner anterior aspect, excise perhaps three inches of fractured bone. . . ."

Dan looked at Townsend's hands, blood and other things crusted beneath the fingernails. "I'm obliged, sir, but no."

"You'll die."

"Then at least I'll go to heaven or hell with both legs."

Townsend turned to the bearers. "Come, lads, take him up gently."

Dan produced the revolver and cocked the hammer. "I'll shoot whoever lays a hand on me."

The bearers froze.

"You damned young fool!" growled the surgeon. "Give me that pistol!"

Dan kept it leveled.

"Keep it and die then!" Townsend dismissed the bearers and glared at Dan. "I should let you lie there and suffer till you get some sense, but I'll let you have opium balls. Nurse, see to it." He stomped on through the ward, attending to other patients.

"Dan," ventured Lydia as he slipped the revolver under the mattress. "You and Christy can live at the mill. There'd be things you could do. . . ."

The leg hurt so much, Dan almost wished it was off. He gritted his teeth. "I'm not going to be a burden, Lydy. Now, you two go look after the other men that need it." He patted her hand. "I'm lucky to have you both here."

"I'll bring your opium and some coffee and soup," Ellen said, and smoothed back his hair.

Dan kept watch on the surgeon and braced himself for another argument when Townsend doubled back toward him, instead of leaving the room.

"You do understand, Corporal," Townsend said, "that your behavior is going to get you reduced to private?"

"That's the least of my worries, sir."

"Even for an Irishman, you've got a thick head."

Dan grinned. "Maybe that's why the bullet just grazed me."

Townsend shrugged. "I've been wanting to try the water cure on a serious wound," he said gruffly. "Will you consent to the treatment?"

"What is it?"

"Suspicious?" There was actually a twinkle in Townsend's eye. "It's simple. Clean lint covers the wound and clean cold water is poured on it three or four times a day. The wound is covered with cloth to keep the water from evaporating and air from getting in. Both North and South have had good results with the treatment. I've used it, but never on a wound like yours." He added disgustedly: "The other patients all had better sense."

"How many of them died?"

The surgeon's ruddy skin went even redder. "About half," he admitted. "It's more for this treatment . . . about sixty percent . . . with excisions of both tibia and fibula."

"Well then, sir, I can't see that I'm being too foolish. If I let you try the cold water, will you promise not to sneak off my leg?"

Townsend sighed. "I promise. But if you change your mind. . . ."

"I won't."

As Townsend explained the treatment in greater detail, Ellen returned with a tray and a pill. Townsend instructed

176

Ellen that Dan could have opium as needed, and gave Dan half a smile, saying: "Good luck, Private O'Brien. I advise you to give that pistol back to the friend who left it with you, before he gets in trouble."

"Thank you, sir," said Dan.

Lydia had written a letter to this patient's mother. She looked up and saw in the dim lamplight of the hospital tent that his lips were trembling. That was how David had looked as a child when he was trying not to cry. But this lad's bowels protruded.

"Ma'am . . . ma'am! I'm scared. . . ." She knelt beside him, gathering his head against her, murmuring that he would soon see those he loved, it would be joyful with no pain or grief forever.

When his last breath escaped, she kissed him, drew the sheet over the face that had the faintest down, and went to the next bed.

"Water," moaned an older man. "Please, give me a drink of water."

She did, and bathed his wounded thigh. On to the curly-headed youngster whose jaw was shot away. All night and day she worked, all the next night till the head nurse commanded her to sleep. As she huddled in a blanket under a wagon, she gave thanks she was able to help, that she, Lydia Parks of the neat quilt corners, could now sew up wounds with her tiny stitches.

In proud humility, she gave thanks, too, that she, plain, raw-boned, an old maid, could be the most important person in the world to the men whose life or comfort depended on her, or when she held them as they crossed over.

If only she could have held her younger brother.

CHAPTER ELEVEN

Charlie Ware couldn't believe the change in General Price since he'd ridden up and down the line of his troops at Pea Ridge, encouraging them although he was wounded. Nor did the general, who'd allowed a captured Union officer to be hanged and his men shot at Pilot Knob, resemble the chivalrous victor of Lexington who'd let the defeated commander and his wife ride in Price's carriage.

At six feet two, Price had always been a giant. Now he was a flabby one. He led this expedition into his beloved Missouri in an ambulance drawn by four white mules. Not even his splendid white horse, Bucephalus, could carry his 300 pounds for long, although the general heaved himself into the saddle near Jefferson City to exhort his troops.

At the sight of the United States flag, flying from the Capitol, Charlie's heart constricted. He could never hate it as the flag of the enemy. It was still his flag, just as Thos was still his brother and Dan his friend. In the end, at Jefferson City, Price decided against attacking the 7,000 troops manning five outlying, palisaded forts linked by connecting rifle pits. The ramshackle horde meandered on along the Missouri River, winning small victories and accumulating more rag-tag followers.

Price's Army, Charlie brooded, was as unwieldy as its general. 12,000 cavalrymen divided into three divisions headed by Shelby, Marmaduke, and Fagan, seemed an impressive force. After all, hadn't Jo Shelby led his Iron Brigade clear up Boonville a year ago on a forty-one day raid, burning bridges, wrecking railroads and Union depots?

In spite of his devotion to old Pap Price, Charlie couldn't help but wish Shelby was commanding this Army. 4,000 had no weapons, 1,000 had no horses, and all fourteen cannon were small caliber. Worse yet, the Army spread out for five to six miles, cumbered by 500 creaky old wagons loaded with plunder, and hundreds of cattle, not all of them taken from Unionists. There were orders against looting, but the Army had to live off the country and it was hard to draw a line between necessity and pillage.

This autumn of 1864 had seemed a good time to enter Missouri what with most Union troops sent to the savage fighting in Virginia, Alabama, Tennessee, and Georgia. After several summer battles, Union forces had retreated to Little Rock, where they were said to be on half rations and unlikely to hinder Price. General Kirby Smith, Confederate commander of the Trans-Mississippi Department, had been ordered to send all the infantry in Arkansas and Louisiana across the Mississippi to do something to divert some Union troops from the ferocious struggles in the East.

What could be better than a strike into Missouri? The Union high command didn't care about the rest of Missouri, but whoever held St. Louis controlled the vital traffic above it on the Mississippi and Missouri Rivers.

Price had crossed into Missouri on September 19th, bound for St. Louis with high hopes of gaining most, if not all of Missouri, and recruiting soldiers for the desperate Confederacy. Charlie's highest hope had been that he and Travis Jardine could see Travis's older sister, Yvonne, in St. Louis and get news of Melissa and all of the Jardines. That was one of the worst things about this war—not being able to get letters back and forth—worse than fighting, maggoty food, worn-out shoes, even the trots.

Three years since he'd seen Melissa or his family! To Charlie's bitter disappointment, Price learned that 4,500 infantry, veterans of Vicksburg bound down the Mississippi for Georgia, had been put off their boats to help defend St. Louis. Over 3,000 more men were camped below the city, and regiments from Illinois were on the way. Price had lost 1,500 men in brutal fighting at Pilot Knob, eighty-six miles south of the city. Rather than attack St. Louis, he decided to proceed northeast to take Jefferson City, the capital.

There, once again, Price feared to attack. He easily took Boonville where the Army was welcomed by the mostly pro-Southern citizens on October 11th. And there. . . .

"I still can't believe it," Charlie muttered to Travis as they halted for their noonday meal near a handsome two-story farmhouse surrounded by broad fields. "How could General Price have anything to do with guerrillas who ride in with human scalps tied to their bridles?"

"Pap's got to take whatever help he can get." Travis shrugged. "Anyhow, he wouldn't talk to Bloody Bill Anderson till he and his men got rid of the scalps, and then he just ordered him to blow up bridges on the North Missouri Railroad. Anderson's bunch wiped out one hundred and fifty Federals at Centralia a couple of weeks ago. Maybe that's where the scalps came from."

Charlie shivered. "I don't know, Trav. That hair on Bloody Bill's bridle looked like women's hair to me." He changed the subject. "All we've done on this jaunter is wreck the country we pass through. I don't suppose we'll even try to tackle Kansas City or Leavenworth."

"We traveled too slow. General Curtis, who whupped us at Pea Ridge, is in front of us with his Army of the Border." Trav, for once, looked sober. "General Pleasanton's on our rear . . . he was the Federal cavalry commander at Gettys-

burg, remember. Nine thousand of those Vicksburg veterans are marching toward our left. About all Pap can do is
retreat south through Kansas." His brown eyes glinted with
irrepressible high spirits. "I hope we get a chance at the Red
Legs or that damned Doc Jennison!"

Charlie swallowed the last of his water-soaked hardtack
and jumped to his feet. "Look! Sergeant Matthias is firing
the house!"

"Must have found out it belongs to a Union man."

"I'm going to make sure there's no one in the house,
hiding." Charlie broke into a run. He still remembered a
charred body he'd found dragged about by hogs near a fired
cabin. The man had not quite been dead.

Matthias lit a torch in the fireplace, held it under a stool
and bench. One of his squad yanked towels and all manner
of ironed linen goods from shelves in a cupboard, shook
them out, and tossed them and an embroidered tablecloth
over the benches.

"That'll do." Matthias lit another torch. "Get yourself
some fire, men. Bedrooms are fun."

Charlie pelted up the stairs ahead of them, ran through
the four bedrooms, peering under beds, yanking open
chests and wardrobes. In the last room he entered, Matthias
pulled back a counterpane, heaped pillows in the middle of
the great carved bed, stuck the torch among the pillows,
and pulled up the coverlet. Charlie raced back to the first
room he'd searched, the one that looked like a girl's, all
pink and white. Maybe not too old of a girl. An elegant doll
smiled from the ruffled pillows on the canopied bed. A
white robe and nightgown hung from pegs behind the door.
Charlie leaned out the window and threw the doll as far as
he could into some bushes.

"Yank down the drapes and pile 'em on!" called

Matthias, dragging a featherbed out of a chest in the next room. "Damn' Union trash won't put this fire out."

Where were they? Charlie thought. *Somewhere close. The cornbread on the table was still warm. Likely hiding out in the trees. Could they see their house burn?*

"No silver and such," grunted Matthias. He had run down the steps in front of Charlie and was ransacking a china cabinet while smoke and flame furled from the kitchen. "Bet they buried it some place. Get out of here, boys! Look around for sign of fresh digging."

Beyond a half dozen slave cabins, each with its garden patch, was a fenced graveyard. Most of the sunken mounds were grown over, but at the far end was a raw red mound with a little wooden cross.

"Bet their silver and jewelry and all's hid there!" yelled the sergeant. He grabbed a pitchfork from beside a shed, thrust it down. There was a dull *thunk*. "Didn't bury it very deep!" he crowed. Moving the fork to one side, he sunk the tines, tossed away clods, dug deeply again. This time he brought up the edge of a box. A colored woman burst out of the cornfield.

"Cap'n, for Lord's sake, leave my baby be!"

"Baby!" Matthias snorted. He set the box on the ground, held it with his foot, and worked a tine under the lid, prying up one edge, then another, shaking off the woman who clung, weeping, to his arm. Forcing the lid back, he grasped the edge of a piece of cloth. It matched the dress the doll wore, the doll Charlie had thrown into the bushes. Something dropped from the swaddling. The woman caught the infant.

Before he turned away, retching at the smell, Charlie glimpsed a small face underground things had been at, and a mass of springy black curls.

"Maybe there's stuff underneath," persisted Matthias. He started to use the pitchfork again, but Charlie caught his arm.

"There's the bugle! Come on, Sarge. There's nothing here but dead folks."

But he hoped the girl was alive, and her family, and that she'd find her doll.

CHAPTER TWELVE

On that late October morning, the clouds in the east looked like white paving stones crumbling at the edges. A rich harvest had come from the seed corn rescued last fall from Lafe Ballard's gang. Christy gave thanks as she hefted sacks of grain into the wagon. There was so much corn that, rather than take over a few bags at a time on Lass, Christy had decided to take the team to the mill.

With the aching question of whether Charlie and Travis were still with Price, she'd heard about that general's rampage across Missouri from the Parkses and young Will Hawkins, who had recovered and visited whenever his captain would let him. Will scarcely limped on the leg Sarah had set, and he was glad to chop wood or do other chores, if he was asked to dinner. Sarah, with mischief in her eyes, always gave him honey.

Anyway, Price was now fighting his way west along the Missouri. How strange and terrible it was to wonder if her brother and Travis might come as invaders through their homeland! Of course, either or both might have died of wounds or sickness any time these past three years. Christy breathed a prayer for them and tried not to think of their appearing on the border as enemies. If Price came this way, it would be well to have the corn ground and most of it stored in the valley.

Sarah came from the cabin with a crock of honeycomb tucked against her with her good arm. The other had a sprained wrist, which was why she was minding little Jon, instead of going to the mill. Jon clambered down the step and lurched along beside her, grasping her skirt to steady nine-month-old legs. He hadn't seen the wagon before; it had been hidden in the woods ever since Christy had driven it home from Sedalia.

He tried to bite the spokes, and would have toddled under Lad's hoofs if Christy hadn't grabbed him. She sat down on a stump and opened the bodice of her blue dress, the one made of Dan's gingham, her only unpatched garment although faded from many washings. Jon could eat mush and mashed fruit and vegetables, but he still loved his mother's milk. He set his summer-browned fists against her breast and his cheek dimpled as he suckled blissfully.

Watching him, Sarah laughed. "Reminds me of what Will Hawkins said about that hard-drinking sergeant of his . . . 'If he was as fond of his mother's milk as he is of tanglefoot, he must of been almighty hard to wean.' "

Christy laughed and promised: "I'll leave the corn, wagon, and Lad, and come straight home on Lass. I'll go back for the meal when Mister Parks has it ground. Or if he has meal on hand, I'll swap for it."

"Don't rush. Have a visit with Susie and Harriet." Sarah lodged the crock securely among the sacks. "Jonny likes applesauce, and there's maple syrup for his mush. He won't starve."

"Yes, but. . . ."

"You haven't been out of shouting distance of him since he was born." Sarah's sniff was almost unnoticeable, but it was a sniff. "A change'll do you both good."

Christy didn't argue as she kissed her son's red-brown curls and gave him to Sarah who scooped him up with her sound arm. How could Christy not love him with all her heart when he was so like the men she loved best in the world, Dan and her father, and yet was so much his own new self?

Blue Boy begged to go with her. At her gesture, he jumped into the wagon, nimble in spite of the withered paw that had healed but was almost useless. In spite of that, he lorded it over the remaining hounds. As Christy drove off, she ached that her father would never know his namesake and that her mother and Dan were missing his babyhood. Still, what she'd told Dan was true. Jon adored Noelle, only two years older, and both had Beth, Mary, and Richie for idols and playmates. He had love, training, wisdom, and laughter from Hester, Star, Lilah, and Sarah. But, oh, if only his father were home!

His last letter had been dated mid-August. His leg was still draining and the surgeon wanted to keep him in the hospital, but he was determined to start home on Raven. *I could travel faster by train and boat, sweetheart, but then I'd have to get home from Leavenworth or Sedalia or Rolla. Besides, the bullet Raven took from that bushwhacker ruined him for a battery horse. He was turned out to live or die, but Thos and Harry looked after him. So Raven and I will come home together. Don't you fear! After all this, nothing's going to keep me from seeing you and our boy.*

The letter before that had told about Davie Parks and, enclosed, had been the signet ring from Richie's brother. After the war, they'd have to find out if the relative in Tahlequah was still alive, in spite of all the raids and fighting in the region. On the same day Price had invaded Missouri, Stand Watie and a Texas brigade had captured a Union train of 300 wagons bound from Fort Scott to Fort Gibson with food, clothing, medicine, guns, and ammunition for the soldiers and refugee Indians. Those supplies and the 740 mules were a windfall to the Confederates who hustled them to the southern part of Indian Territory—where Confederate Indian refugees huddled as miserably as Union ones did at Gibson or southern Kansas.

Indian Territory couldn't be in much better shape than the wasteland of western Missouri. The Burnt District, they called it since Order Number 11, had finished the work of Border Ruffians, jayhawkers, Union troops, and guerrillas. Soldiers on both sides would come home to find cabins, barns, and fences burned, livestock stolen, families scattered. How many would or could start over here?

As she neared the mill, she saw plumes of smoke to the north that looked like fires along the Military Road, not just smoke from chimneys. Alarmed, she clucked to the horses. She could see the mill now. The buildings looked as usual, but Zephyr and Breeze weren't in their pasture, no chickens pecked in the barnyard, and there were no pigs in the pen. Surprisingly the cows grazed peacefully along the slope.

Now she could see that many horsemen had been here since it rained three days ago. Hoofs had chewed up the turf. Feathers from luckless chickens fluttered in the brush near ashes of several cook fires. Crows pecked at the heads of Simeon's prized Yorkshires. Flies swarmed on their hides and hoofs.

The sights and smells called up memories of the slaughter of animals at the Ware farm and Rose Haven. Fighting nausea, Christy drove the wagon into the barn. Price's Army, or some of it, must have passed through. They seemed to be gone, but stragglers would be glad of good horses. Anyway, if Union troops were in pursuit, they might need fresh horses, but Christy was not of a mind to supply them.

Susie answered her knock, four-year-old Andy peeking from behind at her right while his cousin of the same age,

Danny, peered from the left. Harriet clutched a poker. Nine-year-old Letty gripped a club-like limb, doubtless snatched from the kindling box.

"Christy!" Susie drew her in. "If you rode Lass, it's a mercy you didn't come while Price's men were here! They'd have stolen her like they did Breeze."

"Did they hurt anyone?"

"Not really, though Missus Morrison worked herself into hysterics and is in bed with one of those headaches that last for days. Papa and Catriona were in bed with ague, and Owen had ridden Zephyr to join the militia at Sugar Mound. He came home after the battle to tell us he was all right. . . ."

Christy's heart squeezed tight in her chest. *Charlie? Travis?* "There . . . there was a battle?"

Letty rested the poker on the floor. Her blue eyes were big. "We heard the cannons while we were having breakfast. The dishes rattled on the table!"

"Our men caught up with the Rebels by Mine Creek day before yesterday," Susie said, her eyes lit with un-Quaker like pride. "They outnumbered our men three to one and had cannon, but Pleasanton's cavalry charged so hard, the Confederates broke after a mêlée."

"Our boys trounced them so thoroughly, Price had to forget about taking Fort Scott," put in Harriet. "He was whipped at Westport on the Twenty-Third, and skedaddled this way. Folks say there must have been twenty-five thousand Rebels scattered all over the prairies the night of the Twenty-Fourth. Of course, most were just rabble . . . hungry, ragged, stealing everything they could eat, wear, or carry off."

Christy shut her eyes. Bad enough to think of Charlie as one of a regular Army; far worse to imagine him acting like a bushwhacker or the Union soldiers who'd carried out Order Number 11. She really would rather see him dead!

"They dug our potatoes and turnips," Susie enumerated, "roasted the chickens and pigs, and ran the mill all night, grinding our wheat and corn and all the grain people had left with us." Wrathful spots burned in Susie's cheeks. "Over a thousand pounds they carried off in our wagon, hitched to Breeze, but that wasn't enough! They came in the house and would have shaken the last flour out of the barrel, except their captain made them give us about five pounds, and he made them leave half a ham when they raided the smokehouse."

"I'd just churned and made six blocks of butter," Harriet said, glancing at the scrubbed, empty wooden frame. "I couldn't keep from crying when they took it, so they gave me back one block."

"It's a marvel they didn't take the cows or eat them," puzzled Christy.

"Oh, they had lots of beef on the hoof and hundreds of wagons," said Harriet. "Over at Trading Post, they butchered three hundred head, but, when they heard General Curtis was on their heels, they left the carcasses and cleared out . . . not before they burned the store and looted, though. They stole everything the Nickelses had, but Doc Jennison caught one thief and hung him in the Nickelses' barn."

"An officer tucked a bag of grain under a baby's pillow and soldiers let it be," added Susie. "The captain who was here said he was sorry to take our flour and food, but he knew supplies would be sent to us in a week or so while he and his men had a long way to go."

"Owen went back to help bury the dead from both sides," Harriet explained. "One hundred and fifty Union soldiers are being buried at Mound City. The Rebels will be buried on the battlefield or wherever they fell in the retreat, way over three hundred of them. More were wounded, nine hundred taken prisoner, and Price lost eight cannons and lots of supplies. General Marmaduke surrendered to a young private. If it weren't for Jo Shelby's brigade, Owen says the Rebels would have had it a lot worse. Shelby guarded the fords while the others came across."

"Yes"—Susie nodded—"and those wagons that slowed down their army the whole month of the foray and got stuck at Mine Creek so the men couldn't get across before our cavalry came up . . . well, Price ordered most of those wagons burned as soon as what was left of his men crossed the Marmaton. Except for Shelby's brigade, it's not an Army now, just a mob." Susie paused. Regret deepened her voice. "Price may get some new recruits back to Arkansas, but they're not armed or trained. All he really did in the state he loves so well is lay waste to the countryside for sixty miles along his line of march, and stain his reputation by accepting help from the likes of Bloody Bill Anderson, Quantrill, and George Todd."

Bloody Bill? Christy remembered the scalps on Bill Anderson's bridle, the knotted silk cord. It had to be the same person; yet, to her, he would always be the handsome, blue-eyed, young man whose voice softened when he spoke of his sister Josie. Josie, crushed with three other girls in the collapsed jail in Kansas City. It seemed to Christy that, at least along this border, there was more wrong than right on both sides.

"The meeting house in Mound City was turned into a hospital," Harriet added. "The Wattles women, Amanda Way, and a lot of other women nursed both Rebels and our men. I went over and helped yesterday till ambulances came to take the wounded back to Leavenworth."

"You . . . you didn't see my brother Charlie or Travis Jardine?"

Susie's face stiffened. "Oh, Christy!" She put her arms around her. "Oh, my dear, we weren't thinking. . . . No, I didn't see either Charlie or Travis."

No one said what they were all thinking: that the two could be among the hundreds of Confederate dead shoveled into mass graves along Sugar Creek.

Harriet shook her head. "We're sorry, honey. How dreadful for you to have brothers on both sides."

Christy straightened. "That's happened in a lot of families. It's worse for Mother. We just have to pray they come home safe and can be brothers again." She swallowed hard. "Is there any way I can help you here?"

"Thank you, but we're managing." Susie's smile was faint, but she did smile, and tousled Andy's bright hair. "After all, the Rebels cleaned our cupboards out for us and there's no grain to grind."

"There's my wagonload of corn. You can have all you need."

"I'm sure Papa will appreciate that. We'll pay you back when we can. Harriet, let's help Christy unload."

"I'll drive over to the mill," Christy said.

When the bags were stored inside and Christy was leaving, Susie pressed her hand. "I'll ask Owen about Charlie and Travis," she promised. "If we hear anything, we'll let you know. Owen is sure he can put together a wagon from wrecked ones left on the battlefield. After he gets your corn ground, we'll use the oxen to bring your meal over." She sighed. "Poor Breeze! I hope he breaks away and comes home. Zephyr won't know what to do without him. They've been together since they were colts."

"Don't get your hopes up," Harriet advised. "You know Owen said there were hundreds of wounded horses lying on the field or galloping around it in panic. They trampled scores of the dead and wounded."

"Dear God! I wish animals didn't get slaughtered in our wars!" Christy said, thinking of Jed and Queenie stolen so long ago, and knowing their chances of being alive now were slim. She blinked back tears to think of the dark-faced ewes, and Patches and Evalina, the Poland Chinas who had suckled their piglets with such pleasure. She also remembered Raven, wounded and turned out to die. "I hope Mister Parks and the ladies get well quickly," she told her friends. "Tell Owen there's no hurry with the corn."

Susie hugged the crock of honey. "At least this should finish the war in Missouri and the border. General Curtis and General Blunt are chasing Price. They won't stop till they run him into Southern Arkansas. He won't be back . . . and neither will anyone else." She called after the creaking wagon: "When Dan comes home, let us know right away!"

"I will!" Christy shouted back, and drove past the scattered remains of the pigs without looking.

She intended to drive the team to the woods near the Ware home, unhitch and unharness them there, and leave the wagon, but Sarah ran to meet her at the edge of the clearing.

"Christy! Christy! Dan's home!"

CHAPTER THIRTEEN

Sarah climbed into the wagon and took the reins. "Go on in! I'll hide the team and wagon. Dan's fevered and his leg's ugly. We'd better get him to Star and Hester."

Christy flew into the rear cabin. Dan lay on her bed—their bed. Sarah had cut away his pant leg. Corruption oozed from the inflamed puckered wound. Dark lashes lay against bones that drew the skin taut above cheeks that showed hollows even under a short curly red beard. A cup, bowl, and basin with a towel were on a stool. Jon sat on the rug, examining his father's battered forage hat.

Sinking on her knees, Christy kissed Dan's cracked, dry lips. "Danny! You're home!"

His eyes opened, those eyes he'd given Jon. "Home to stay, darlin'." She could tell the words and smile took effort. He raised a hand to her cheek. "Sorry Raven and me look so rough, but, now we can quit traveling, we'll soon be worth our feed."

"You are anyway!" She hugged him the best she could. The stench of the leg came through his odor of smoke, sweat, and grime. "Oh Dan! I've prayed and dreamed and hoped . . . I can't believe you're here!"

"Neither can I, sweetheart." His fingers tangled in her hair. "And to finally clap eyes on our boy! He didn't know what to make of me at first, but he quit crying when I let him have my hat."

"He doesn't see many strang. . . ." Christy broke off.

"Well, I am a stranger." Dan chuckled. "We've got all

the time in the world for him to get to know me. If I'd been fussed over by so many womenfolk, especially my mama, I don't think I'd much like a big old geezer moving in."

Sarah came in with the teapot, poured him another cup of the honey-sweetened willow tea, and held it to Dan's mouth while Christy raised him. "I think you're better already, Corporal," Sarah told him.

"Seeing Christy's better than any medicine, but I'm just a plain old private again." He held up his arm. His eyes danced with some of their old zest. "See where I lost my bars for telling the surgeon he couldn't saw off my leg? Howsomever, ladies, as of June Twentieth, Congress voted us a magnificent raise of three dollars a month for a grand total of sixteen!"

"You're still in the Army?" Christy couldn't keep fear out of her voice.

"Not for long," he assured her. "Surgeon Townsend wrote the surgeon at Leavenworth. When I can ride, I'll report there to be mustered out. No hurry. I cut Price's trail on the way here. Just as soon wait till he's long gone."

"He is . . . or will be as fast as he can." Christy told of the havoc inflicted by the retreating Rebels, and their crushing at Mine Creek. "There could be stragglers. As soon as you've rested a little, Dan, we'd better get you and the horses to the valley. Star and Hester can do more for your leg, and for Raven, too, than we can."

Dan sighed. "I'd like to sleep a month, wake up all better, and then. . . ." He grinned wickedly at Christy.

She blushed. Warmth stirred within her, almost like a quickening child. Dan's wound and emaciation filled her with protectiveness, but now his gaze made her aware of him as a man, as her lover. That was like the promise of a feast after years of starvation.

Sarah watched them with amused sympathy and a touch of wistfulness. "You've kept your mush and tea down all right," she said. "How about a bowl of Tom-fuller? While you eat, I'll put a slippery elm poultice on that leg."

"And I'll feed the baby." For Jon had dropped his father's cap to pull at Christy's arm—her breasts were full.

She started to go in the next room.

"Please give our laddie his dinner here," Dan said.

So, feeling oddly shy, she opened her dress and cradled Jonny. She loved the feeling of her milk flowing into him, a link between their bodies, although she no longer carried him under her heart.

"Greedy little cuss!" At Christy's affronted look, Dan gave a tender laugh. "Oh Christy, darlin'! The two of you are the fairest sight to ever bless my eyes! Wait'll I get my hands on my fiddle. I'll make you both a song." His eyes darkened. "I've a song for Davie in my head and must work that out, too."

"The Parkses will like that," Christy said, and thought: *I hope your mother met you, Davie, and you're happy now wherever you are.*

Sarah used a clean, ragged towel to fasten the mass of dampened elm bark over the wound. "Can you keep low against one of the horse's necks so you can ride through the passage?" she asked. "Skinny as you are, you'd be quite a load for Christy and me to manage."

"I'll ride low," Dan said. "I've done it often enough when we hauled our gun into position. I hate to ride Raven. The poor fellow's tired. But if I'm not on him, he might panic in the cavern."

"You ride him. I'll bring Lass, and Christy can carry the baby. One of us can come back for Lad. We'd better plan to hole up for a while."

"I know one guerrilla who won't come through again,"

195

Dan said. "Wasn't it Bill Anderson you took care of when he was shot?"

Christy nodded. A wave of dread swept through her.

"Some Union troops caught up with his bunch," said Dan. "Anderson was killed and. . . ." Seeing Christy's face, he broke off. "You had a kindness for him."

"He probably kept us from being burned out. And . . . he told me about his sisters." Dan didn't speak. "What happened to Bill?" she pressed.

"The soldiers cut off his head and stuck it up on a telegraph pole."

"Good God!"

"You've got to remember that on top of plenty of killings, he and his men took twenty-three unarmed Union soldiers . . . some wounded . . . off the train at Centralia and made them strip, then slaughtered them."

"I know, but. . . ."

"We'd better go," Sarah prompted. "I'll bring Raven up to the door and then fetch Lad." She picked up Dan's hat, holstered revolver, and brogans. "Best not leave anything to show a soldier was here." She hesitated. "I'd like to take the hounds. When Lige comes home, he'll be sad enough about Sam and the others without these getting killed."

"Blue Boy's so slowed down by his leg, he can't catch anything," said Christy. "Chita and the others sort of do what he does. If Star worries about the 'coons or 'possums, we can tie the dogs up. Shouldn't be for long. In a week or so, the last of Price's rabble ought to be out of here."

Christy walked ahead with a candle lantern, Jonny settled on one hip. She had cried out with pity when she saw Raven, shoulder leaking foul-smelling pus, once glossy hide scruffy and dull. He lipped an apple from Dan's hand, though, and set out willingly although he shambled. "I wish we could tell him he can rest in the valley," Christy said. For some reason, she thought of her father reading from *Le Mort d'Arthur*. "And heal himself of his grievous wound. Like you, Danny."

"Sure." He reached to touch her hair, then leaned against Raven's mane as they entered the cavern. "Hester and Star will fix us up. But I think I'd get well just from being home with you."

Sarah was behind them with another lantern, bringing Lad, the sound of his hoofs muffled by the soft padding of the dogs.

When they finally reached the broad opening and blew out one candle, Dan slid down from the saddle and steadied himself with the its horn. "Ladies, I'm staying here till whoever fetches Lass comes back."

"But. . . ."

"Star and Hester can begin on me right here," he pointed out. "But I'm watching this passage till everybody's safe."

Christy looked at his revolver that he had belted on. "Don't shoot unless you have to. It could bring down the roof of the cavern."

"I'll go back for Lass," offered Sarah. "But first I'll lead Raven and Lad down."

"I'll take Jon to the women and tell them about Dan," said Christy. She kissed her husband's bearded jaw. "Then I'll come back and wait with you." She helped him settle against a boulder, picked Jonny up again, and turned at a strangled cry.

"Drat and dog-gone it!" gasped Sarah, looking up from where she'd fallen at the bottom of the rocks. Tears glistened in her eyes. "A hundred times I've been down this cliff, but today I have to twist my stupid ankle!" She tested it and grimaced. "I hope I haven't broken it."

"You'd better ride Raven to the house," Christy urged.

She slipped the halter off Lad and gave him a slap on the rump before she helped Sarah mount.

"I can take the baby." Sarah reached for him. "You hurry and bring Lass back so we can get your husband to a proper bed."

The women and children had come out of the bark long house. Christy waved and scrambled back to the entrance. "You're soon going to have more help than you'll want," she teased Dan.

They kissed hungrily, with longing, thankfulness, and promise. She picked up the lantern and moved into the eternal night of the cave.

Christy blew out the candle, paused at the opening of the cavern as she always did, and scanned the cabin, outbuildings, harvested fields, and pastures across the creek. Wild geese called from a shimmering wedge high above. Flaming maples, sumac, and russet oaks blazed among cedars and pines. The great walnut by the cabin had lost its nesting summer birds but was a splendor of gold.

Birds and wild creatures had missed some clusters of grapes on the huge grapevine tangling up the white-limbed sycamore at the creek crossing. The papaws beside it looked ripe. Christy decided to take a basket of wild fruit to Dan. She wanted to look over the cabin, anyway, before shutting it up.

She entered the main cabin. Coming in out of the sun made it dark inside. It was a moment before she noticed the man sitting at the table, eating from a bowl. His back was to her. He wore a blue uniform, but many of Price's men did, either for disguise or because their own clothes were in rags. Heart tripping, Christy wondered if she could creep out unseen. Then the man turned, rising in the same instant, sweeping his hat off silver hair.

"Your Tom-fuller would be tastier with meat." Lafe Ballard smiled, showing small white teeth. "I was sure you'd not grudge some to an old neighbor."

"Were you with Price?"

"Till he burned the wagons on the other side of the Marmaton. I've no taste for being chased clear to Arkansas by the damned bluebellies. Reckoned I'd come home and see if Ma can give me any money before I head West."

"I think she's gone to stay with relations."

"We don't have any." Lafe closed the space between them. He was between her, the poker, the ash shovel, or the iron skillet, anything she could use as a weapon. "Ma, I reckon, is somewhere in that cave you just came out of . . . or on the other side of it."

He'd seen her. Tongue dry as burned cotton in her mouth, Christy said: "We . . . we just store things there. . . ."

"I'll look for myself." He drew something from his pocket. "You see, my dear, I found this under your bed." He held out a yellow button and moved closer. "Since there were no cobwebs to show this has been there a long time, I take it to mean a Union soldier's been here. Recently." With his toe, he nudged a grimy pus-soaked bandage. "From this, also fallen under the bed, I surmise the blue-belly was wounded." He set his hands on her shoulders. "My guess is your Irisher's dragged himself home and you've hidden him in that most interesting cave."

"He has a revolver," Christy warned.

"Bless you, so do I, two of them as you see. And I have two loaded cylinders, a little guerrilla trick. There's also a shotgun in my saddle scabbard . . . my horse is in your barn enjoying your corn . . . but I shouldn't need that."

His brand on her wrist felt seared anew. Her flesh prickled beneath his hands. It was like being toyed with by a giant cat. "Go away, Lafe! Don't grieve your mother more than you already have."

"I want to grieve her. I want to make her sorry she ever had me."

"What made you like you are? How can you be Hester's son?"

"I wonder that myself." He stepped back.

Chill eyes swept her from head to foot. The ice-burn spread from her wrist through her, paralyzed her mind. Somehow she had always known this time would come, just as she knew someday she must die.

Lafe's amused smile changed and his voice thickened. "I wonder why I've never got you out of me." Again he came closer, forcing her head back, and brutally took her mouth. Slow, numbing poison spread through her, but a detached part of her brain whispered: *Don't fight him now. Wait till he's off guard.* . . . She almost fell as he pushed her away from him, mouth twisting.

"You're nursing that damned brat I felt kick in you last time!" He rubbed the fingers that had closed on her breast on his trousers to wipe off the milk. "I wish to hell I'd ridden him out of you!"

She started to drift toward the poker, but he caught her. "I'm not giving up on you. I'll leave you while I go tend to Dan . . . or could it be your brother, Thos? Whichever, when I bring you his head, it should hurt you so much that your pain'll overcome my disgust. If it doesn't. . . ." The pupils of his eyes spread over pallid irises. "Then I'll have to take my pleasure out of doing other things to you. I could start by cutting off your breasts. Seeing how milk looks mixed with blood."

She wrenched free, dodged, almost grasped the poker when his fist crashed into her jaw. Lightning exploded in her head.

★ ★ ★

Dazed as she regained consciousness, Christy tried to touch her aching jaw and found her hands were tied behind her. She remembered then, tried to sit up, and fell back. Her arms were bound to her sides by strips of sheet that went all the way around her. Her ankles were pinioned. Lafe hadn't bothered with a gag. There was no one to hear.

Thank God, Dan had his revolver. But Lafe was tricky. If Dan used up his six shots, he'd have no chance to load again. If only she could come up behind Lafe with a butcher knife or poker. . . .

Frantically wriggling her ankles and wrists, she found no give in the knots. She swung her legs off the bed, thrusting her upper body erect. After several attempts, she managed to stand, but was too tightly bound to shuffle. In spite of the way her hands were fastened tightly behind her so that she couldn't use her elbows to crawl, perhaps she could snake across the floor to the fireplace and burn some of the knots enough to tear them apart.

She knelt and dropped on her side, rolled on her belly. Thrusting herself along by toes and hips was excruciatingly slow. She rolled. Much better! The door to the dogtrot was open. So was the one across it.

Ah! She'd forgotten about the axe beside the stacked wood. She'd rather get cut than burned. Leaning sideways against the blade, she frayed the sheet between her arm and side, worked back and forth till the cloth split.

Now she could get her wrists on either side of the blade and see-saw. Why hadn't she sharpened the axe when she noticed it was getting dull? This is taking so long!

The knots gave way. Her wrists were scraped and bruised, tingly from hampered blood flow. She was clumsy in using the axe to free her ankles, but at last she was free!

Racing through the kitchen, she snatched up butcher knife and poker and ran for the cave.

Lafe had taken the lantern, but she'd been through the underground way so often that she thought she could avoid the drop-offs even without a light. How long had he been gone? How long had she been unconscious? Christy ran in smooth places, slowed where she had to sense her way around the river. She doubted she could catch up before he reached the entrance, but, if she could steal up on him, she'd kill him if she could—drag his body out and bury him so Hester would never know.

After what seemed forever she glimpsed the firefly glow of the lantern. Soon, beyond it, glowed the distant oval of blue, blue sky.

If she shouted now, surely Dan would hear her. It would warn him and startle Lafe. But it might also set off vibrations that would violate the silent world of the cave, bring stalactites or ceilings crashing down. Dan, in the entrance, should be safe, but as for herself and Lafe. . . .

She drew in her breath. "Dan!" she cried. "Lafe's here! La-a-afe!"

The lantern stopped, as if set down. There was no sound as she ran except the pound of her heart in her ears.

Then Hester's voice pealed, echoing through the passage, magnified by every formation. "I remember now, Lafe! *You* hanged Emil Franz. Go! Go away from here. . . ." Like one demented, she began to scream, shrieking like the voice of the long-suffering, outraged earth.

A groaning reverberated in the cave. Christy ran for her life. Bullets crashed. In front of her, to one side, Lafe ducked behind a boulder. He and Dan fired again in the same instant. Before Lafe could shoot again, the cave's muted protest broke into a thunder of plummeting rock.

It buried Lafe. A single cry broke off, echoed and reëchoed, before the rocks settled. Some pelted Christy as she raced for Dan, but nothing large hit her. From the passage behind came rumblings and sounds as if hundreds of windows were shattering. Then she was at Dan's side.

Blood trickled through his fingers as he gripped his shoulder. "It's not much," he assured Christy. "See to Hester."

Hester was trying to wrench the stones away that had buried her son. Christy helped her shoulder several to the side. When they saw Lafe's crushed head, there was little to be done till a horse could be brought to drag off the fallen chunks.

"Did my voice bring it down?" Hester sobbed.

"I'm sure my bullets caused it," Dan told her.

"When I yelled, I heard something begin." Christy tried to put her arms around Hester, but the older woman knelt in silence a moment, and then got to her feet.

"I tried to pretend he wasn't mean when he was little and liked to torment things. I told myself he couldn't have anything to do with my second husband's getting killed. I made myself forget about Emil." Her eerily steady voice broke. "But he was still my little boy once. God forgive him."

"Amen," said Dan and Christy in one breath.

Before Dan let the women dress his shoulder, he kissed Christy long and hard. "As soon as you've plugged me up," he said, "let's go down to our son."

Allie and Sarah, with Lass hitched to a rope, helped Hester clear away enough rocks to free Lafe. It was possible for people on foot to thread their way through fallen rocks and stalactites to the other side of the cavern, so the women carried Lafe home and buried him under a tree he would have loved to play in when he was little.

Hester didn't speak of him after that, but Richie clearly became more than ever her son as he was in the days of his innocence, as well as the grandson she'd never have.

So successful was Star's and Hester's treatment that, in ten days, Dan could get around with a crutch of peeled apple wood. His gaunt face and body were filling out. The children's hero, he told funny stories and sang marching songs with the ribaldry toned down, but what everyone loved was for him to play his fiddle. He managed to do this for short spells in spite of his wounded shoulder.

After Jon's first wide-eyed alarm at this tall scratchy-faced man creature who claimed all too much of his mother's attention, the child decided it was nice to curl up in his father's arms and nap against the thump of his heart. He learned fathers can whistle and trot babies on their good knee. In short, he quickly turned into daddy's boy, except when he was hungry or very tired and cross. His jabberings, accidental or not, began to have a recurring "Da-Da" oftener than his first refrain of "Ma-Ma".

Christy was anxious about Lass. When she announced her intention of bringing the mare through the other passage—the one Hildy had used to enter the valley—Dan insisted on going with her. Sarah wanted to check her bees and Allie was anxious about her cabin and the tannery vats, so they all went.

"I hope there'll be something for Ethan and the boys to come home to," Allie said as they came out of the dark passage.

"There is," Dan said. He grinned at her questioning look. "Oh, Allie, Allie! There's you and Mary!"

"Ethan can use our oxen and horses to plow till you can

get some more," Christy said. "And we can give you a cow, calves, and some chickens. Look at all the help you gave us when we settled here."

"And I'll give you some bee gums," Sarah promised.

Allie smiled through tears. "It's going to be good to really be neighbors again!" As soon as they crossed the creek, she started for her home through the splendor of autumn leaves.

Christy froze as the three of them neared the cabin, going slow to accommodate Dan's limp. "Look! Two strange horses in the pasture with Lass!"

Dan drew his revolver. The cabin door opened. A tall, thin man in butternut stood there. He lowered his shotgun.

"Christy!"

They ran to meet each other, brother and sister, but as they met in a laughing, weeping embrace, Charlie held her back and asked: "Where's Melissa? Where's Mother? How did Father die? I found his stone."

"And my folks?" Travis's eyes no longer danced. "We've been to Rose Haven."

First assuring them that Ellen Ware was safe when last heard from and that Melissa and Joely were well and in St. Louis, Christy explained all that had happened, faltering now and then.

"We couldn't imagine what had become of you," Charlie said after a hushed moment. "But the cabin wasn't burned or ransacked and Lass was in the pasture so we thought we'd rest and wait a few days. Figured you'd maybe gone to the Parkses during Price's retreat, but we were nervous about riding there, in case Union soldiers were around."

Travis slanted an oblique look at Dan who'd sat down to ease his leg. "Looks like one is."

"Not for long." Dan shrugged. "I'm mustering out as

soon as I can travel to Leavenworth."

"Our war's over, too." Charlie gazed at things Christy couldn't see. "Pap Price furloughed lots of the Missouri boys. He knows we won't be catching up with him."

"No use starving out another winter south in Arkansas." Travis's tone was bitter. "There's still skirmishing in Indian Territory, but the fight's really over west of the Mississippi."

"The South is whipped," said Charlie. "Lee and his generals will fight to the last in Virginia and Georgia, but the Confederacy's out of weapons and supplies . . . everything but spirit."

"I'm out of that," said Travis flatly. "Taking up with the likes of Bloody Bill and Quantrill's more than I can stomach, let alone acting like damned jayhawkers."

He looked at Christy. How long ago it seemed since they had danced at Charlie's wedding! How long ago, a life ago, since he had stolen that kiss! "I'm glad you're well, Christy," he said, "and that your man's come home."

"I'm glad you're home, too, Travis."

He shook his head. "It's not home any more, and it'll be less that once the Union has its foot on our necks." He turned to his brother-in-law. "Charlie, do you want to head West with me, or are you of a mind to stay here? Seeing as how the rest of your family's Union, it should be easier for you."

Christy listened with her heart in her mouth. *Please stay, Charlie, please!* But remembering how Melissa had mourned Rose Haven and the life that could never be again, Christy wasn't surprised when her brother said: "That depends on what Melissa wants."

"Why don't one of you borrow my uniform and go see her?" suggested Dan. "Matter of fact, I've got an extra shirt, and they gave me the first overcoat I was ever issued there at the hospital. Ought to be enough clothes to let you both look like furloughed soldiers."

"I want to see Beth first," said Charlie. "Wish I could see Mother, but, if we do go West, I'll get back to see her . . . all of you."

"There's someone in the valley you need to meet, Travis." Christy told him about Lilah and his little daughter.

The startled look on his face turned to pleasure, then to dismay. "But I can't. . . ."

"Lilah's whiter than I am," Sarah adjured him. "You're lucky, Travis Jardine, to have such a sweet, brave, beautiful lady in love with you! And Noelle! Wait till you see her!"

Charlie nodded. "Melissa and Lilah grew up together. They'd be company for each other, if Melissa wants to move away . . . and I'm pretty sure she will. She's probably had enough of Yvonne's company to last the rest of her life."

"Come along," invited Sarah. "I'll take you to the valley."

Christy sat down beside Dan, watching the others out of sight. "It's going to be different," she sighed. "But I'm glad they're safe. Now if Thos and Mother were home. . . ."

"They will be, sweetheart. So will everyone, I'd bet, before another autumn." He took her in his arms. "I love the valley and everybody there," he murmured against her throat. "But you know, honey, it's good to be alone. Do you think maybe . . . ?"

"I think for sure." She kept her arm around him as they went, together, into the happy house.

EPILOGUE

The meeting house at Trading Post was packed, so Dan stood at the back of the room with seven-year-old Jon and other younger men, including his brother-in-law, Thos. Ellen Ware held her dark-haired, four-year-old namesake, Ellen Bridget, while Christy lulled Thos David. Not quite a year old, he didn't appreciate so many strangers and being kept on his mother's lap, but he was tired and she hoped he'd soon go to sleep.

He'd have plenty of children to frolic with as he grew up. Lydia Parks McRae cradled her youngest, while her husband, a cavalry major she'd nursed back to life, proudly held their three-year-old. He sat, no shame to him, because, although he got around fairly well on his artificial leg and a cane, he couldn't stand for long periods. Harriet and Owen Parks had a two-year-old boy. They looked too young to be the parents of seventeen-year-old Letty, who just a week ago had married the much younger brother of Major McRae, come out from Indiana to assist his brother in his law practice.

Beth Ware was sixteen. How swiftly they grew up! She and Luke Hayes were courting. Matthew had died at Shiloh, but Ethan and Mark came home safely. Mark couldn't settle down and had gone West just like Charlie, Melissa, Travis, and Lilah, and many, many more. Mary Hayes was keeping company with a young blacksmith who had taken over the Franzes' old place. Caxtons and

Madduxes had never returned. Lige and Sarah Morrow had moved to the valley, and there Star was helping them rear their three young children.

Daniel Owen Parks and his same-aged cousin, Andy McHugh, stood as quietly as eleven-year-olds could manage, near Owen and Andy's stepfather, Captain Aldridge. This handsome Ohioan, a former Army surgeon now in practice at Mound City, won Susie two years ago after a long, insistent courtship, and Catriona's death, which had perhaps freed Susie of any guilt for taking a new husband. In the full bloom of her early thirties, Susie was expecting the captain's child soon.

Hildy sat next to Hester with Lou, one of the twins born to her and Justus more than a year ago. Hester held Jonathan, who would be the second Jonathan Ware since Hildy and Justus had asked if they might take Ware for a last name. Justus and several comrades from his regiment had formed a freighting company and were prospering.

Now and then, Hester glanced back to see that Richie, her golden boy, was behaving. He was, of course, under the strict but kindly eye of his adoptive father, Simeon Parks, who, to the approval of family and friends, had wedded Hester a few days before the war ended.

As old Hughie Huston rose to introduce Colonel James Montgomery, Christy's gaze roved over those she knew less well. Sam Nickel stood between the two sons left of the six who'd served with their father in the 6th Kansas. Near the front sat the Hall brothers, Austin and Amos, who'd survived the slaughter of Marais des Cygnes by feigning death. Beside Mrs. Nickel was Mrs. Harvey Smith, once Mrs. Colpetzer, who'd driven a wagon to aid the victims and found her own husband dead. Including Dan and Owen, there must be, at this meeting, a score of those who had ridden with Montgomery after the murderers.

Thank God, those days were done, although Christy wished Jennison had not fared so well from his plundering. He owned an opulent saloon in Leavenworth, and his show-place stock farm, a few miles south of there, boasted the best of cattle, swine, and horses. As one newspaper said: *For some five or six years the Colonel enjoyed unusual facilities for selecting fast horses from numerous stables.* He had just been elected to the Kansas State Senate. As for James Lane, depressed and in poor health, the senator killed himself the year after the war ended.

Quantrill got his death wound in one of the last skirmishes of the Civil War, out in Kentucky, and died in a military hospital. Jesse James, Frank James, and their cousins, the Youngers, who had ridden with Quantrill, turned to robbery.

The Burned District was green again with grain, orchards, and pastures. Some blackened chimneys stood like huge gravestones, but many new cabins rose on old foundations. The wounds of the border war might be like Dan's leg, still draining, although he did a man's full work, but Beth's generation was growing up. To her children, the war would seem long ago.

"Let us rise." The war had broken Colonel Montgomery's health. His beard and hair were gray, but his eyes were piercing as ever. "We will sing 'The Battle Hymn of the Republic'."

The room reverberated with Howe's words, but in Christy's mind ran the original song: "John Brown's body lies a-moldering in the grave." When the congregation was seated, Montgomery read the text. *Be not deceived. God is not mocked; for whatsoever a man soweth, that shall he also reap.*

He preached that communities and nations are as subject to the laws of God as are individuals. Even small children were held by his voice. No one nodded during that sermon.

At last he paused to search the faces of his neighbors and those who had ridden with him to quell the Border Ruffians. "I call on my old friends to remember what I said at a sorrowful meeting almost fourteen years ago. I prophesied that the remaining years of slavery could be numbered upon the fingers of one hand, and that during that time I would lead a host of Negro soldiers, dressed in the national uniform, in the redemption of our country and the Negro race from the curse of slavery.

"Brothers and sisters, I believe that with us tonight are the spirits of those who died for our country . . . your fathers, brothers, sons, sweethearts, and husbands. They fought a good fight. They finished their course. In our hearts, they can never die.

"Let us give thanks for them, for their courage and devotion. Let us give thanks we had them as long as we did, and let us rededicate ourselves to ever waging their war for freedom."

He held out his arms. That smile of great sweetness touched his mouth. "Dearly beloved, let us pray."

When the O'Briens and Wares got home that night, Dan got out his fiddle and played his song, the seasons of his life from Irish lullabies through war, hate, and love. And then, with Jonny leaning against his knee and Christy's eyes on him, he played the seasons of peace.

AUTHOR'S NOTE

A marvelous history of the Osages, their beliefs, customs, and way of living, is *The Osages: Children of the Middle Waters* by John Joseph Mathews, himself an Osage. The Osage homelands were once in what are now Missouri, Kansas, Arkansas and Oklahoma, and parts of neighboring states. As white settlers invaded, these lands shrank to a reservation in Kansas, and this dwindled to their last reservation, now Osage County, Oklahoma, over in Indian Territory. More of their history is found in *The Imperial Osages* by Gilbert C. Din and Abraham P. Nasatir. I wish also to thank my old friend, writer Fred Grove, who is Osage, Sioux, and French, for his information on guerrillas and their tactics, and also his encouragement.

Thomas Goodrich's *Bloody Dawn* is a graphic account of the Lawrence massacre. *Early Days of Fort Scott* by C. W. Goodlander is an eyewitness account of the fort, the town, and that strategic corner of Kansas from 1858 to 1870. It was fascinating to visit the fort, and it was in the cannon exhibit that I finally could understand how they were loaded and fired. *The Chronicles of Kansas*, bound volumes of the publications of the Kansas Historical Society, have yielded much enriching material, especially memoirs of the Civil War and pioneer life.

On a misty day of fresh green April, we sought out Marais des Cygnes Kansas State Historical Site. Although it was closed, Curator Brad Wohllhof kindly came up to let us in the small cabin and explain the exhibits that memorialize the murders in that peaceful copse. The fascinating Trading

Post Museum was only a few miles away and there Curator Alice Widner explained many of the rare artifacts, photos, and records donated to the museum by the families of some of the people in this book.

At the Linn County Historical Museum at Pleasonton, Oklahoma, May Earnest, curator, answered many questions and pointed out things of special interest. The Baxter Springs Museum in Baxter Springs, also in Kansas, has spirited murals, period rooms, weapons, clothing, and household furnishings of the Civil War times. It is good to find local history preserved in these museums, often staffed by volunteers. I thank them for their graciousness and help in bringing life to the pages of this trilogy.

Special thanks to my cousin Francis Billings and her husband Albert, who has immersed himself in the Civil War. They live in historic Warrensburg and took me to Lexington where we explored that famous battlefield. Al also hunted up elusive details on weapons. He and Fran did Fort Scott, Pea Ridge, and parts of the Old Military Road with me and have been interested in this trilogy since the idea first entered my mind.

My dear friend, June Wylie of Austin, valiantly undertook driving us through Kansas, Missouri, and Arkansas, tracking down places I needed to see. I am grateful for her help, exemplary patience, humor, and a friendship that has endured half a lifetime.

I hope my great-great-grandfathers, fighting on opposing sides, would think I did them a measure of justice. Even more, I hope the women of those days would believe I tried to tell their stories.

JEANNE WILLIAMS
Cave Creek Canyon
2004

ABOUT THE AUTHOR

JEANNE WILLIAMS was borne in Elkhart, Kansas, a small town along the Santa Fe Trail. In 1952 she enrolled at the University of Oklahoma where she majored in history and attended Foster-Harris's writing classes. Her writing career began as a contributor to pulp magazines in which she eventually published more than seventy Western, fantasy, and women's stories. Over the same period, she produced thirteen novels set in the West for the young adult audience, including *The Horsetalker* (1961) and *Freedom Trail* (1973), both of which won the Spur Award from the Western Writers of America. Her first Western historical romance, *A Lady Bought with Rifles*, was published in 1976 and sold 600,000 copies in mass merchandise paperback editions. Her historical novels display a wide variety of settings and solidly researched historical backgrounds such as the proslavery forces in Kansas in *Daughter of the Sword* (1979), or the history of Arizona from the 1840s through contemporary times in her Arizona trilogy— *The Valiant Women* (1980), which won a Spur Award, *Harvest of Fury* (1981), and *The Mating of Hawks* (1982). Her heroines are various: a traveling seamstress in *Lady of No Man's Land* (1988), a schoolteacher in *No Roof but Heaven* (1990), a young girl heading up a family of four orphans in *Home Mountain* (1990) which won the Spur Award for Best Novel of the West for that year. She was also the recipient of the Levi Straus Saddleman Award. The authentic historical level of her writing distinguishes her among her peers, and her works have set standards for those who follow in her path.